HAUNTED CANADA
GHOST STORIES

PAT HANCOCK
AND
ALLAN GOULD

Illustrations by
Andrej Krystoforski

Stories in this collection originally appeared in
Grim and Ghostly Stories and *Strange and Spooky Stories*.

Scholastic Canada Ltd.
Toronto New York London Auckland Sydney
Mexico City New Delhi Hong Kong Buenos Aires

Scholastic Canada Ltd.
604 King Street West, Toronto, Ontario M5V 1E1, Canada

Scholastic Inc.
557 Broadway, New York, NY 10012, USA

Scholastic Australia Pty Limited
PO Box 579, Gosford, NSW 2250, Australia

Scholastic New Zealand Limited
Private Bag 94407, Botany, Manukau 2163, New Zealand

Scholastic Children's Books
Euston House, 24 Eversholt Street, London NW1 1DB, UK

www.scholastic.ca

Library and Archives Canada Cataloguing in Publication
Hancock, Pat
[Short stories. Selections]
Haunted Canada ghost stories / by Pat Hancock and
Allan Gould ; illustrated by Andrej Krystoforski.
(Haunted Canada)
ISBN 978-1-4431-2894-0 (pbk.)
1. Children's stories, Canadian (English). 2. Ghost
stories, Canadian (English). 3. Horror tales, Canadian
(English). I. Gould, Allan, 1944-, author II. Krystoforski,
Andrej, 1943-, illustrator III. Title.
PS8565.A5695A6 2014   jC813'.54   C2013-905964-4

6 5 4 3 2 1   Printed in Canada 139   14 15 16 17 18

CONTENTS

THE SLEEPING BOY

"Hey, my movie just died," a young woman sitting in the third row grumbled.

"Mine too," someone called from a few seats back. "I think we've lost power in these outlets."

"And I've just lost what I was working on," a young man with a laptop protested. "Hey, driver. What's going on? Is the wireless connection gone too?"

"Yeah, where's the Wi-Fi?" someone yelled from the back of the bus. "What are you going to do about it?"

"And my phone won't work."

The driver could tell people were getting upset but at the moment, internet connections were the least of his worries. He was having trouble controlling the bus.

The passengers near the front were the first to notice. Two men in the seats closest to the door began to nudge each other and whisper. A woman in the second row told the child beside her to sit up straight.

Gripping the steering wheel with one white-knuckled hand, the driver flipped on the loudspeaker with the other.

"May I have your attention, please?"

"Fix the power."

"Shut up."

"Shhhhh, be quiet."

Finally the din faded to a low murmur and the driver tried again.

"Ladies and gentlemen, sorry about your devices, but right now we've got a bigger problem."

Although his heart was racing, he tried to look relaxed. He didn't want the passengers to sense how worried he was.

He took a deep breath and continued. "The engine seems to be losing a bit of power. Now, it's nothing to worry about. I just want you to know, that's all, so you won't be surprised if I have to pull over. If I do, would you kindly stay in your seats until I give you further instructions? And, uh, how about we just forget about movies and e-mails for the moment?"

Then he leaned forward, focusing intently on the mountainous highway ahead. This was a difficult stretch of road — about thirty kilometres of twists, turns and steep grades before it linked up with the Trans-Canada. Definitely not a great place to run into problems.

At least the road was bare and dry. It had been two weeks since the last snow, and crews had long since finished sanding and ploughing. Still, even under ideal conditions, a big vehicle like the bus needed full engine power to keep rolling. And right now, no matter how hard he pressed the accelerator, the bus was losing speed.

With dusk falling, the driver didn't want to be stranded at the side of a mountain highway with twenty cold, hungry, angry passengers. It might take hours to get a replacement bus. And that was assuming he could even get in touch with head office.

He'd first noticed the trouble on the last long, steep grade. The bus had definitely lost power.

But what had really hardened the knot of fear that was forming in the pit of his stomach was the way the bus had headed into the oncoming lane — all on its own. In vain, he had wrestled with the steering wheel, trying to pull it back to the right.

He'd panicked briefly as they'd approached the crest of the hill. Was another bus, car or truck thundering to meet them head on?

Mercifully, the lane had been clear. But, as the bus coasted down the other side, still on the wrong side of the road, his fear grew.

He wasn't the only one who was scared. One of the two men in the front seats leaned over and asked quietly, "Are you having trouble with the steering?"

Before he could answer, an older woman farther back called out, "Driver, shouldn't we get out of the passing lane now?"

Other voices joined in.

"Come on, mister. Get over."

Once again, he flipped on the loudspeaker.

"Okay, folks, could we keep it down a bit, please? No point in getting everyone upset."

He paused until the bus was quiet, then went on.

"Look, I'm going to give it to you straight. I'm having a little trouble steering this baby. She's got a mind of her own at the moment. But we're still on the road, and we're obviously not speeding, so . . . Holy cow! Hold on!"

Without warning, the bus lurched forward, then fishtailed. For an agonizing moment, it slid sideways along the highway.

Finally, it came to rest, pointing directly at a snow-covered side road. Then it began to move again — straight up the narrow road.

Pandemonium broke out behind the driver. Screams of fear filled the bus. A child started crying. Some adults did, too. One woman began to pray.

"I've had it," bellowed a man in a checked jacket. He

picked his way up the aisle over the jumble of bags and coats that had spilled out of the overhead luggage compartments. "Who do you think you are? Where'd you learn to drive?" he shouted when he reached the driver.

"Look, mister," the driver shouted back. "What do you see?"

He held his hands in the air as the steering wheel swung first to the right, then to the left, all on its own.

"And there?" he continued, pointing to his feet. They were planted firmly on the floor, not on the pedals. "I'm not driving this thing, buddy. I wish I were."

Horrified, the man backed up and fell into the doorwell. He pushed himself up and began to pound on the doors.

"Stop the bus! Let me out," he shrieked.

"Take it easy, fella. I'd stop if I could, believe me. I want out just as much as you do."

News of what was going on spread among the passengers like wildfire. Many of them began to shout and cry. A young woman slipped out of her seat, crouched down on the top step, and began to talk quietly to the frantic man at the door. At the same time, the driver started talking over the PA system again.

"Please, everybody, stay in your seats," he pleaded, trying desperately to sound calm. The last thing he needed was a busload of hysterical passengers. He already had enough on his mind.

He cleared his throat and went on, "Look, I don't know what's happening any more than you do. The doors won't open. The steering wheel is useless, and so are the brake and accelerator. It seems somebody has us under remote control."

He swallowed hard, trying to control the quaver in his voice. "I'll keep doing what I can. But it would really help if you would try to stay calm. I know that's not easy. But if we panic, somebody is bound to be hurt. So far, nobody has been. And whoever — or whatever — is driving this bus is at least keeping us on the road. See? We're bouncing along nice and slow."

A fresh chorus of shrieks broke out as the bus swerved round a bend. It skittered off a pile of snow a plough had left at the roadside, then straightened out and went on.

Over the clamour, the driver tried to make a comforting joke. "So, maybe he — or it — is new on the job, right?"

When nobody laughed, he continued. "Look, I know this road. We're on our way to Silver Lake — whether we like it or not. Someone will be there to give us a hand. Say, how about a little song? I bet the kids would like a song."

Clearing his throat, he began to sing in a deep voice.

"My eyes are dim, I cannot see . . ."

A few others joined in weakly.

"I have not got my specs with me . . ."

The chorus grew steadily louder until most of the passengers were singing nervously.

"I have not got my specs with me."

As they sang, the bus bounced forward jerkily, slithering on the bends but always clinging to the road.

An uneasy calm settled over the passengers. Most of them sat quietly, glancing out the windows or staring at the back of the seat ahead.

The driver had stopped trying to fight the nightmare. Still, he kept his hands lightly on the steering wheel and a foot poised over the brake pedal, just in case things returned to normal.

Suddenly, the bus rounded a bend and the village of Silver Lake lay ahead. A dozen or so low, wooden buildings lined its short main street. A ski lodge was nestled on a tree-lined slope above the village.

Between the trees in the distance, the setting sun reflected off the icy surface of a lake. It was a beautiful, peaceful scene except for one thing — the short street was jammed with traffic.

Some of the passengers began to clap while others gave a half-hearted cheer as the bus rolled slowly up the street, then came to an abrupt halt in front of a small general store. And there it stayed, right in the middle of the road.

"Now what?" the driver said to no one in particular. Outside, a crowd was gathering, waving to the passengers inside.

Cautiously, the driver reached for the lever that controlled the doors. He pulled it back, and was surprised to hear the familiar "whoosh" as the doors parted.

Gingerly, he tapped the horn. The loud honk startled the people in front of the bus. He grinned sheepishly and waved an apology. Then he stood and faced his passengers.

"Well, folks, I guess this is the end of the line. Let's see if we can find out what's going on."

As an afterthought, he started to add in his official voice, "And don't leave any valuables on the bus. Blueway is not responsible for . . ."

Before he could finish, people leaped from their seats and pushed past him. Like every good captain, he waited until the last passenger was safely off. Then he left, too.

The scene outside was confused. A truck driver gestured wildly as he described his experience to the crowd.

"There we were, totally unable to do anything and . . ."

A woman in a turquoise ski suit interrupted.

"We were picked up. I swear it. My husband says I'm imagining things but, believe me, something picked up our van — the silver one over there — and moved it. Moved it right off the lane up to our chalet and onto the main road. Then it pushed us back into town, too."

"That's ridiculous," sneered the passenger in the checked coat. "You must have skidded on some ice. Made it seem as if you were airborne, that's all."

"The road was bare," the woman shot back huffily.

"You pulling our legs, lady?" another man asked.

A tall, grey-haired man stepped forward and said, "Well, I'm not, and the same thing happened to me and my wife. That's our Chevy over there."

The bus driver moved up beside him. "I'm not kidding around either. Mind you, we weren't picked up or anything. But we were . . . pushed. That's how it felt — as if something was pushing us around like a toy."

"This is crazy. I'm getting out of here," a voice shouted.

Others joined in the chorus.

"Me, too."

"Yeah, come on. Let's go."

"Don't go — not yet."

The bus driver swung around. The last voice had come from behind him.

"Who said, 'Don't go'?" he asked.

"I did." An old man wearing a leather hat with fur ear-flaps jostled his way through the crowd. His grizzled beard rested on a wool scarf tucked inside the collar of his parka.

"Don't go yet," he pleaded. "It's not safe. Can't be. Otherwise he wouldn't have brought you here."

"Your brain's frozen, old man," one of the bus passengers yelled.

A woman pushed her way to the old man's side.

"Just a minute," she said firmly. "Don't you talk to Seth that way. He knows this area like the back of his hand. Show some respect. Now, Seth, what did you say?"

"He brought them here. Something's wrong somewhere and he brought them. Wait and see."

"Who's 'he'?" the driver asked.

"Yes, Seth. Who is 'he'?" the woman asked gently.

Silence had fallen over the crowd. Everyone was listening now, waiting to hear what the old man would say.

"The boy."

"What boy? Where?"

"The Sleeping Boy."

"The Sleeping Boy? Seth, what are you talking about?" Now even the woman was beginning to sound skeptical. "The only Sleeping Boy I know is the island in the lake."

"Yep, that's him," the old man nodded, clamping an old brown pipe between his teeth.

The woman turned to the driver and explained.

"There's a small island in the middle of the lake —

beyond the trees, that way." She pointed into the darkness. "It's hard to see it now that the sun's gone down. Besides, it just looks like a huge lump of snow at the moment. The first settlers along the lake called it The Sleeping Boy because that's what it looks like from shore. The name stuck.

"People have been making up stories about it ever since. They say it's the body of a boy who got separated from his father when they went out to check their traplines. For days, he wandered, trying to keep warm at night by burrowing under the snow.

"One morning, he didn't wake up. When spring came and the snow melted, there he was, asleep in the middle of the lake. Legend has it that he lies there waiting for his father to find him and take him home."

The old man nodded as the woman talked. When she finished, he spoke again.

"True enough. But he wakes up sometimes."

"Oh, Seth. That's just a very old, very silly story," the woman said kindly.

Turning back to the driver, she continued, "There are some who say that the boy wakes up every now and then, just before something terrible is about to happen. They say he guards these hills, making sure no one comes to grief the way he did."

Another man pushed his way to the front of the crowd.

"Hogwash," he snorted. "I've lived here nearly as long as Seth and I don't believe a word of it. It's all rubbish."

He turned to face Seth and the woman.

"Why don't you tell them the one about how he wakes up every spring and pushes chunks of ice around on the lake like toy boats?" he asked sarcastically. "They say he's playing with them.

"Or how about the one that has him hanging around the animals — bears, badgers, groundhogs and the like. That's supposed to be why they wake up in spring — to play with him. Now that's a good one, don't you think?"

The crowd began to grow restless, laughing when a young man pointed at Seth and gestured that he was out of his mind.

"You're right there, fella," the man snickered. Then he stomped over to the store, yanked open the door and disappeared inside.

"What about the forest fire?" Seth asked.

"Oh, Seth. That was just a coincidence," the woman said.

"Coincidence, you say? Not a cloud in the sky. People ready to move out because the fire was licking at the edge of town. And suddenly, a deluge. Right on the fire and nowhere else."

"Seth, that happened seventy years ago. People exaggerate over the years."

"Maybe so, but I was here then. Saw it myself with my own two eyes. And the train trestle. I was here then, too."

"What about the trestle?" the driver asked.

"Collapsed. Crashed right into the gorge. But the train — the one that was supposed to be on it right at that moment — was safe. The Boy stopped it, just short of the trestle. Then he pushed it back around the bend, all the way to the station. Nobody was hurt. The Boy made sure of that."

The woman looked confused.

"He's lost it," someone muttered.

The old man turned slowly until he was staring directly into the eyes of the speaker.

"Maybe so. Maybe so. But I wouldn't try to leave just yet if I were you. You're safe here. You'll see."

Then they heard it — a low distant rumble at first. It grew louder and louder until it erupted into a deafening roar. The ground vibrated under their feet.

"Avalanche!" someone screamed. People stood, open-mouthed, staring over the treetops as an enormous snowy white cloud mushroomed into the darkening sky.

Finally, the roar faded to a faint echo. Still, the crowd stood in stunned silence.

The woman from the van found her voice. "That was over near our chalet," she said softly.

"And out by the highway," the bus driver added.

"Thanks, Boy," the old man said, looking up at the star-filled sky. He turned and began to walk away.

People cleared a path to let him pass. Then they, too, looked up at the sky — many offering their own silent thank you to The Sleeping Boy of Silver Lake.

GOLDEN EYES

Ashley had been speechless when her parents had given her a horse on her thirteenth birthday.

"For my very own?" she had finally sputtered, still thinking she must be dreaming.

"What are you going to call him?" her dad had asked.

"Sam," Ashley had answered quickly, certain that the strawberry roan would be a faithful companion, just like Frodo's Sam in *The Lord of the Rings*. "We'll go everywhere together!"

And go everywhere they did. Whenever she could, Ashley would saddle up Sam and head off with him to the places she'd been with her dad when she was learning to ride.

Once she had ridden Sam all the way to Duck Lake, and, another time, they'd gone as far as Dead Man's Hill. Today she was heading into the badlands for a close-up look at some hoodoos, fantastic pillars of layered rock that jutted out of the moon-like barrens.

It had taken major persuading to get her parents to let her go. They were nervous about her ranging so far from home.

"What if something goes wrong and you need help?" her mother had argued. "Hardly anybody lives out there."

"And those coulees can be pretty confusing. You could get turned around and never find your way out," her father had added.

Finally, though, they'd agreed. But only after Ashley had assured them that Sam never forgot the way back, and that she'd take extra food and water and a compass, just in case she got lost.

The sun was high overhead by the time Ashley and Sam reached the edge of the badlands. The grass had steadily grown patchier, and they'd spent the last ten minutes picking their way carefully across a couple of the barren coulees that had been gouged into the prairie landscape by retreating glaciers.

It was hot and Sam needed a rest. So did Ashley's rear end. A grove of spindly aspens clinging to the bank of an ancient, nearly dry creek offered the promise of a little shade and a drink for Sam.

Ashley tethered her horse so he could reach the trickle of water in the creek, took a sandwich out of her saddlebag, and sat down in the thin shade of one of the trees. Chewing slowly, she let her mind wander, imagining all sorts of exciting adventures that she and Sam might have out here in this weird, stark landscape.

Sam noticed the change in the weather first. His neighing snapped her out of her daydreams. She looked up. Sam was tossing his head to the right, then looking back at her. Off in the distance Ashley saw what was worrying him. Thick black clouds were rolling in from the west and the fragile aspens were starting to sway in a strengthening breeze.

Ashley scrambled up, brushed herself off, and moved toward her horse.

"Good boy," she murmured, rubbing his velvety muzzle affectionately. Then she dug her jacket out of the saddlebag. "Just in case the weather changes," her mother would say whenever she checked to see if Ashley had it with her. The wind is really picking up, Ashley thought as she zipped it up. Seconds later, the sun disappeared behind the clouds and she heard the first distant rumble of thunder. A flash of sheet lightning followed.

Ashley scanned the threatening sky and made a face. There was no avoiding a good soaking — unless she could find shelter. Going farther west wasn't an option. She'd just be heading straight into the storm — and deeper into the badlands. Not much shelter there. Besides, she wanted to go home.

First, though, she had to get away from the trees. Whipped by fierce gusts of wind, they looked like they were about to snap and come crashing down. They also made perfect lightning rods.

She swung up onto Sam, checked her compass and nudged him back in the direction they'd come.

Sam maintained a steady pace, never faltering even when a blinding fork of lightning cut a jagged path to earth just ahead. Soon after, the first huge drops of rain splattered Ashley's jacket.

Ashley crammed her hat more tightly onto her head and hunkered down into her jacket. This didn't stop cold trickles of water from finding their way down her neck to her T-shirt.

She tried to guide Sam in the right direction but, eventually, she gave up. The rain had become so heavy that it was impossible to see more than a few metres ahead.

She'd have to trust Sam and simply hope that the two of them would stumble on help. She bent lower, hugged the horse's neck, and gave him his head.

Sam was picking his way slowly along what seemed to be the rocky bottom of a shallow coulee when Ashley thought she spotted something. She peered through the rain and waited for the next lightning flash to make sure. There it was again, off to the left — the outline of a shed or shack.

"Come on, buddy," Ashley urged, reaching forward to pat Sam's neck. If anything, though, the horse began to slow down. Ashley dug in her heels and Sam kept going, but barely. As they neared the small building, he came to a dead stop. He wouldn't go any closer.

The rain eased a little, enough so that Ashley could make out more than an outline. Not much more, though, because there wasn't much more to see. Only two walls of what looked like a small house remained standing. Two walls and a chimney. The rest was a shell. Its charred, wet remains glistened in the murky light of the storm.

"No shelter here, Sam," Ashley said. "Let's get a move on."

Then she saw her, right in front of the burned-out cabin. She was tall and thin, and she seemed to be waving. Ashley rubbed the rain from her eyes and looked again. She was still there.

What's this girl doing way out here by herself? Ashley asked herself. Maybe she needs help, too. She kneed Sam forward, but the horse wouldn't budge.

It took some serious urging to get Sam moving. And then, when they got closer, he nearly bolted.

"Easy, boy, easy," Ashley soothed, grasping the reins firmly.

Now that she was close to the girl, she was glad that she'd decided to try to help. She looked about Ashley's age and she was eerily pale. Her long, dark hair was plastered against her cheeks, and her clothes — a yellow shirt and jeans — were dripping wet. But it was her eyes that made the most impact. Even in the poor light, Ashley could see that they were golden.

She'd never met anyone with golden eyes before. What's more, when the girl looked at her, Ashley felt as if those eyes could see right through her.

"Are you okay?" Ashley began nervously. She couldn't think of anything else to say.

The stranger nodded and reached out.

"You want a ride?"

Again, she nodded.

Her response was accompanied by another rumble of thunder, farther away this time. Still, she reacted with a jolt, her eyes filling with fear.

"Okay, hop on," Ashley said, holding out her hand. The thin girl grabbed it and Ashley pulled her up behind. She didn't have to worry about Sam handling the extra weight. The girl was amazingly light, wet clothes and all. Still, Ashley thought she felt Sam tremble a little as she settled in.

Now what? she thought. I'm not sure how to get out of here and, if she knows, she's not saying.

As if reading Ashley's mind, the girl tapped her arm and pointed to the right. Squinting through the rain, Ashley thought she could make out a narrow track winding upwards out of the coulee.

"You want me to go that way?"

She felt the bent head nod against her shoulder.

"Okay, you don't have to talk, but I'm Ashley Robbins. Just so you know. Hold on."

Sam needed little prompting this time, moving toward the track as soon as Ashley flicked the reins.

Gradually, the rain wound down to a fine drizzle until, finally, it stopped altogether. Then the setting sun broke through the clouds behind them, casting a fiery glow on the drenched countryside.

"Red sky at night, sailor's delight," Ashley said, feeling a little foolish as she tried once more to make conversation. "At least I know now we're heading east. I live east of here. Is that where you live, too?" Again, all she felt was a slight nod against her shoulder. That, and the soft breathing on the back of her neck. That was no comfort. If anything, it sent shivers down her spine.

Now that she was starting to dry off a little, Ashley realized it was the strange girl's breath, not the evening air, that was chillingly cold. The realization sent a wave of goosebumps spreading across Ashley's damp shoulders and down her back.

She resisted the urge to turn up the collar of her jacket. She didn't want to upset her mysterious passenger. The whole situation was weird enough already. All she wanted was to get to the girl's house — or wherever they were going — and call home.

Home. Just the thought of it warmed Ashley up a little. Home, and fried eggs and bacon and hash browns. Home, and a soft bed and a cozy quilt. Home, home. Home, home. Her head began to bob in time to the rhythm of Sam's hooves. The last thing she remembered before dozing off was a thin, cold hand moving over hers to grab the reins as they slipped from her grasp.

Later, much later, she awoke to the crunching of gravel and the on-off flashing of a spinning red light. Sam was standing quietly on the shoulder of a paved road and, incredibly, Ashley was still in the saddle.

"Is that you, Ashley?" a voice called. She turned toward it, but was blinded by the headlights of a car. Two strong, warm hands reached up to help her out of the saddle.

"Officer Kovalski," she whispered hoarsely, as her eyes adjusted to the light. "Boy, am I glad to see you."

"Me too, but now we've got to get you home," Kovalski said. "This is Cal's place. Tether your horse to his gate. I'll call and get him to put it in the barn for the night. Your folks can bring the trailer and pick it up in the morning."

"My folks!" Ashley was suddenly frantic. "I have to call them."

"Take it easy, girl," Kovalski gave Sam's reins a tug to make sure she had tied them securely to the fence. "I'll radio in and the dispatcher will call them. They're pretty worried. That freak storm caused a slew of flash floods out in the badlands — and they told us that's where you were headed. The sergeant and Bill are out there now in the four-by-four looking for you."

"Sorry," Ashley mumbled. "I didn't know a storm could come up that fast."

"No harm done," Kovalski said as he opened the door and guided her into the passenger seat of the cruiser.

"Wait!" Ashley suddenly remembered the girl. "Where is she?"

"Who?"

"The girl that was riding with me — the one who showed me the way back."

"No girl around when I found you," Kovalski said, slamming the door.

"Then you'll have to look for her, too," Ashley said. "What if she slipped off after I fell asleep? I can't believe I did that. I just couldn't keep my eyes open."

"There was no sign of any girl, and we've had no missing-person reports — other than you, of course," Kovalski said as he slipped into the driver's seat and started the engine. "No harm, though, in taking a drive down the road to see what we can find. What did she look like?"

"Well, she was about my age, maybe a little younger. And she had long brown hair and golden eyes."

Kovalski stiffened and turned to stare at Ashley. "Golden eyes? What else?"

"Well, she was really skinny and she was wearing a yellow top and jeans. And she was just standing there in the pouring rain in the middle of nowhere. Well, sort of in the middle of nowhere. There was an old cabin, but it looked like it had burned down. All that was left was a chimney and parts of a couple of walls. Why? Do you know her?"

Kovalski looked puzzled, "About your age, right? You're sure?"

"Maybe a little younger. Why?" Ashley repeated.

"Oh, the golden eyes . . ." Kovalski hesitated. "Reminded me of Sarah Jackson. But that's an old case. Happened at least ten years ago. She'd be in her twenties by now — if she survived — so it couldn't have been her. The eyes threw me for a minute. I'd never heard of anyone with golden eyes before Sarah — and, come to think of it, I haven't since."

"What happened?" Ashley was almost afraid to ask.

"She disappeared. Took off into the badlands one day. In fact, there was a flash flood that day, too. After it was over, we searched — but never found any trace of her. These sudden floods can be pretty vicious, the way they come barrelling down the coulees without any warning. We figure she got swept away. Her bones are probably still out there somewhere."

Ashley's stomach tightened. She sat quietly as they drove, scarcely breathing as the meaning of Kovalski's words sank in.

"Her parents moved to High River after that," Kovalski continued. "Ended up leaving their place empty. Nobody was interested in buying it. Pretty unfriendly country there, right on the edge of the badlands. It burned down a few years later."

Kovalski looked at Ashley and shrugged. "End of story."

He reached for the radio and clicked the microphone. "I better call the Sarge and Bill. They've been out there for hours."

As the radio crackled to life, Ashley sat stunned, shivering despite the warm air blasting out of the heater.

"Listen, Bill, I've got the Robbins kid. Found her safe and sound on the road by Cal's place."

"That's good news. Sarge and I will go on in then."

"Catch you back at the station. How's it looking out there, anyway? Much damage?"

"Nah," Ashley heard Bill respond through the static.

"Near as we can tell the only damage was to the ruins of the old Jackson property. And that's no great loss. Looks like the flood swept right through the place and took out everything in its path. There isn't a bush or tree in sight and the ruins are gone. Totally. Good thing the Robbins kid wasn't out here, after all, or she'd be gone, too."

GAME BOY

Steve Filmore ate, drank, slept and lived video games. He spent every spare second with his new system, the DRX7. So it came as no surprise when his math test came back with a big red 43 at the top.

The night before, when he was supposed to be studying, Steve decided to try just one game. One game led to another . . . and another . . . and, suddenly, it was time for bed. The evening had disappeared, swallowed up by the electronic monster.

Now what? he wondered, as he crossed the schoolyard. Mr. Harper had kept him in for "a little chat" about his test result, so the playground was nearly empty. Just as well, too. Steve was in no mood to talk to anybody.

He headed out to the lone tree at the edge of the baseball diamond and flopped down against the trunk. Lately, he'd been hiding out there a lot. It was a great place for playing video games. No one bugged him.

Steve reached into his backpack and dug under his math book to find his DRX7. Within minutes, he was lost in the video game's universe. An entire baseball team could have thundered past and he wouldn't have noticed.

So when the voice broke his concentration, he nearly jumped out of his skin. He hadn't heard anyone coming.

Steve stared at the boy who was crouched beside him looking intently at the small screen. He was definitely a kid, yet his face had the wizened, wrinkled look of an old man.

"What did you say?" Steve asked, tearing his eyes away from the strange-looking face.

"I said, do you have to jump on all those guys?"

"Oh yeah. You have to. You get more points."

"Is it hard?"

"Uh, not once you get the hang of it. After that, the more you play, the better you get."

"I get it. Like math," the boy said, pointing to the textbook.

Steve stared again. This kid doesn't just look old, he thinks old, too, he thought. He must be the only kid on earth who thinks video games are like math.

"No way," Steve said aloud. "This is nothing like math. This is fun."

"I always thought math was fun."

"You're nuts. It sucks."

As Steve spoke, he shut down the game and opened up Tetris.

"What's your name?" he asked as he began to play again.

"Ben."

"Ben who?"

"Ben Farber. What's yours?"

"Stephen Filmore. But call me Steve. Only my mom calls me Stephen."

"I know what you mean. Mine used to call me Benjamin."

"But she doesn't anymore? How'd you get her to stop?"

"Um . . . she just stopped, that's all. You know, you're really lucky to have a game like this. It looks amazing."

"It is. I don't remember seeing you around here before. Are you new?"

"No. I've seen you before, though."

"Oh, but you don't go to this school, right?"

"No, I don't go to this school."

Steve was really concentrating now. The shapes were falling fast and he had to slot them into place quickly. He didn't hear what Ben said next.

"Sorry. What did you say?"

"I asked if you'd let me have a turn sometime," Ben said shyly.

Steve glanced at his watch.

"Oops," he said. "Not today, that's for sure. I've got to get home." He shut down the game and began to pack up. "Besides, in another week, I probably won't be playing it myself."

"What do you mean?" Ben asked.

"Well, Mr. Harper — my math teacher — says he'll tell my folks if I flunk another test."

"But what does that have to do with your game?"

"Are you kidding? If my mom and dad find out I'm flunking tests, they'll take it away. They said they would, and they meant it."

"Oh." Ben frowned, then his face brightened. "Hey, I've got an idea. Suppose you pass your next test . . ."

"Get serious."

"Well, just suppose you do. Then you'd have your game for a while longer at least, right?"

"Yeah. Until I flunk the test after that, anyway."

"But you won't flunk another test. Not if you practise. Math is just like playing video games, really. Once you get the hang of it, you just have to practise to get better.

I was pretty good at math. What grade are you in?"

"Six."

"That's good. I got past that," Ben said.

I would hope so, Steve thought. He looks old enough to be a professor or something. Just really small for his age.

Ben continued, "When's your next test?"

"Monday."

"Okay. How about this? I help you with your math for the rest of the week. If you do better on the next test, you let me use your game for just one night. What do you think?"

"A whole night?" Steve couldn't imagine lending it out for more than five minutes.

"Well, if you don't do well, you might lose it forever. And I would really love to play some of those games, especially that last one. They weren't around when I . . . I mean, where I lived."

"No way. Where were you? On the moon or something?"

"Something like that. Now, what do you say? Is it a deal?"

Steve hesitated, then shrugged. "Okay. What do we do? You wanna come to my house or do you want me to go to yours?"

"Oh . . ." Ben seemed confused. "How about we meet right here after school every day? Behind this tree? You're the only one who ever comes here, and . . ."

"How do you know that?" Steve interrupted sharply. Maybe this wasn't such a good idea after all, he thought. I don't even know this kid. And from the sound of it, he's been watching me.

"Oh . . . uh . . . I've seen you here a few times, that's all. I don't go to school here, but I wish I could."

"Well, why can't you?"

Again, Ben seemed confused. Then he went on.

"Well, my mom and dad had to move here. And the school year had already started, so Mom decided to teach me at home." He paused, as if remembering something, then added, "She used to be a teacher. That's what I wanted to be, too."

"Wow, no school! That would be great."

"It wasn't . . . isn't. It's actually pretty boring."

"Yeah, I guess so," Steve said. "I never thought about that."

"So," Ben said suddenly. "About this math. You've got your books with you. Why don't we start right now?"

"Okay," Steve said reluctantly. "But this is a waste of time. You'll see."

An hour later, he wasn't so sure. Ben was patient and he had a way of coming up with great examples. Decimals were parts of his allowance and fractions were parts of game scores. Steve was surprised when he checked his watch and saw that it was nearly dinnertime.

"I've really got to go," he said, packing his bag.

"Same time tomorrow, then?" Ben suggested hopefully.

"No problem, it's your time that we're wasting," Steve said as he took off across the yard. At the gate, he turned back and shouted, "Hey, thanks," but Ben was nowhere in sight.

The next afternoon, Steve had to help set up chairs for a PTA meeting. It was nearly four o'clock when he headed for the old tree, hoping Ben would still be there.

29

It wasn't until he got right up to the tree and peeked around the trunk that he saw him. Ben was sitting with his hands clasped around his knees, staring at some kids playing Frisbee in the park across the street.

"Hi, Steve," he said without looking up. Then he turned and smiled. "So, our deal is still on?"

"Guess so. But you're the one who's gonna lose out, Ben."

"Let's just see what happens," Ben smiled.

Once more, he helped Steve work through the world of multiplication, division, numerators and denominators.

They met again on Wednesday and Thursday. By Friday, Steve was beginning to think that doing well on a math test just might be more than a dream.

"See," Ben said as they finished up, "it's really not so bad after all, is it?"

Grudgingly, Steve agreed that it wasn't as hard as he'd thought.

"But," Ben warned, "you should try those last questions one more time over the weekend. Don't look at the answers in the back until you're finished. The test is Monday morning, right? When will you get it back?"

"Actually, Mr. Harper said he'd mark mine right away. If I bomb, which I probably will, he said he'll be on the phone to my parents Monday night."

"No way that's gonna happen. You know your stuff now. And I can have your game Monday night?"

"Sure. A deal's a deal. I'll give it to you Monday after school. But just for one night."

"One night," Ben said, beaming. "That's all."

The happy look on Ben's face gave Steve an idea.

"Hey," he said as he packed up his books, "we always have tacos on Friday night. You wanna come to my place for dinner? My folks won't mind. There's always lots, and . . ."

He stopped. Ben's smile had disappeared and, for a moment, it looked like he was about to cry. Then he said lightly, "Nah, but thanks for asking. And don't worry about Monday. You'll ace it, Steve. I know it."

"Sure," Steve said sarcastically. "See ya," he called as he began to jog toward Park Street.

"Goodbye, Steve," Ben said quietly.

"What did you say?" Steve shouted.

"I said good luck," Ben yelled back.

"Thanks," Steve hollered. "I'll need it."

He spent much of the weekend doing homework — not just math, but social studies and English, too. He couldn't believe how much catching up he had to do.

After dinner on Sunday, he went back to his math. When he was unsure about one question — the last and the hardest — he went downstairs to ask for help. His parents were in the living room.

"Hey, could one of you help me with this?" He sat down on the couch and showed them the question.

His dad began to scribble numbers.

"Dad, could you write the percents as fractions of a hundred right at the beginning? That's the way Ben showed me. I can follow it easier."

"Who's Ben?" Mom asked.

"He's just this kid who's been helping me with my math."

"I don't remember you mentioning a Benjamin before."

"Ben, Mom, Ben. And I haven't. He's just this kid I met after school."

"Really? What's his last name? How old is he? And where does he live? Does he go to your school?"

Steve could tell that his mother's Beware of Strangers warning system had just clicked into action.

"Mom, it's fine. He's just a kid, and he's really smart, too. His name is Farber — Ben Farber. He doesn't go to my school — and I never asked him how old he was because I didn't want to hurt his feelings."

"What do you mean?" Dad asked. He'd stopped writing and was listening carefully now, too.

"Well, he's a little shorter than me and he acts like a kid, but he looks kind of old. It's hard to explain."

"What did you say his name was?" Dad asked, looking alarmed.

"Ben Farber."

"You shouldn't joke about Ben," his mother said, pursing her lips. "Besides, how did you hear about him?"

"Mom, what's with you? I'm not joking."

"Okay, then. Did you just make up this story about getting help to impress us? So we won't take your video games away or something?"

Steve was confused. It looked like he was in trouble — and he had no idea why.

"He could have just lucked into the name," Dad said to Mom over Steve's head.

"Yes, but what about what he said about the way he looked?" his mother asked nervously.

"Hey guys, I'm here. Talk to me. What's this all about? Ben's just a kid I met, I tell you. And he just looks a lot older than a kid. A few wrinkles like Granddad, that's all."

"We're being ridiculous," Dad said abruptly. "Let's get back to this problem."

"No, wait." Steve wasn't willing to let it drop. Something strange was happening. "What's wrong?"

"It's nothing, really," Mom said. "It's just that there was a boy named Benjamin Farber who moved here when we were kids. His family wanted to be closer to the medical centre. Ben needed so much special care by then."

"By when? What was wrong with him?"

"Well, we never met him. But our parents told us about him."

"Yes," Dad continued. "He had a very serious — and very rare — disease, one that makes your body grow old in just a few years."

"By the time they moved here, Ben was already too weak to go to school. And apparently he really wanted to. He was just a kid. He wanted to do all the things other kids did."

"He died about six months after they arrived," Mom added. "It was so sad. His parents moved away soon after the funeral. So you can see why we were so surprised by what you said, can't you?"

Steve was stunned. This is crazy, he thought.

"Forget it," Dad said. "It's just a coincidence, that's all. Now let's get back to this problem, shall we?"

Steve sat quietly while Dad finished explaining the math question, but he wasn't paying much attention. As soon as possible, he escaped to his room.

There has to be an explanation, he thought, as he slipped into bed. There just has to be.

By the time he got to school the next morning, he'd convinced himself that Dad was right — it was all just a coincidence.

Steve was surprised when he was one of the first to finish the math test. He was also surprised to find that he'd at least tried every question. A first. Once the test was over, though, the rest of the day seemed to drag endlessly.

When Mr. Harper finally dismissed the class, he asked Steve to stay behind. Steve's heart was pounding as he waited to hear his fate.

"How did you do it, Steve? Congratulations." Mr. Harper handed him his paper. At the top, with a big happy face beside it, was a large blue 81.

"I think you've finally got the basics, Steve. You keep this up and your mark will be much better on your next report."

Steve thanked Mr. Harper and left in a daze. He wandered slowly out to the schoolyard, where he stood staring at the big tree for a long time. There was no sign of Ben.

His head was spinning. If Ben is *the* Ben, I've just spent four days learning math from a ghost. That isn't possible . . . is it? And if it is, how can a ghost play with a game? And he isn't around, anyway. I'd be stupid to leave my DRX7 here. Somebody'll steal it and I'll never see it again.

He spun around and walked quickly toward the gate. You're not real, Ben. You can't be, he said to himself as he began to jog toward home.

His parents took him out for pizza that night. To celebrate the great math mark, they said. When they got back home, Steve said he was tired and went to his room. He lay on his bed, trying to make sense of what had happened.

No matter how hard he tried, though, the one thing he couldn't forget was the smile on Ben's face when he'd agreed to let him have his DRX7 for a night. And his own words kept coming back to him. A deal's a deal, he'd said.

Steve looked at his watch. It was still only eight-thirty. He got up, grabbed his things and headed downstairs.

"I forgot something in the schoolyard," he shouted as he ran out the door. "I'll be right back."

It was nearly dark when he got to the school. He walked slowly across the empty baseball diamond to the tree. No one was there. It's too late, he thought. Ben got tired of waiting. Maybe he even saw me leave after school.

"Ben, I'm sorry," he whispered.

Then, he saw it — the hole in the trunk where kids sometimes hid secret messages. He reached up and felt inside. It was a small space, but big enough. He looked around to make sure no one was watching. Then he set the unit carefully in the hole.

"Here it is, Ben. Have fun," he whispered and walked away.

When he got home, he crawled into bed and fell asleep wondering if he'd ever see his DRX7 again.

The next morning, Steve got to school early. Again, he looked around to make sure he was alone. Then he reached into the hole.

The console was there, exactly where he'd left it. No one

has touched it, he thought. I was too late, after all. Well, at least I've got it back. Somehow, though, this thought didn't make him happy.

He was surprised to find the power turned on. I must have pushed the On button when I grabbed it, he thought. Then he looked at the screen. Under the Game Over message was an incredibly high score.

Steve hit Start. The familiar *Tetris* tune began and there, on the opening screen, were three high scores. The one he'd already seen was listed first, with two others close behind.

Someone had used the game — someone who was a fast learner and a good teacher, too.

"I hope you had fun, Ben," Steve whispered. "It's easy once you get the hang of it, isn't it?" Just like math, he added silently.

Steve turned off the power. As he walked toward the school, he glanced back at the tree. There was nobody there but, just in case, he waved.

A DREAM COME TRUE

Jennifer's voice cut through the silence in the kitchen. "I found it. It's real," she called out happily. Startled, Morgan Ross spilled the coffee he was pouring. He hadn't realized she was back.

"What's real, dear?" he asked, grabbing a paper towel to wipe up the puddle.

"The house, Dad. The one in my dream. I found it all by myself." Jennifer beamed with pride.

"Right — how could I forget?" Morgan muttered under his breath as he dumped the soggy paper towel into the garbage. For the past nine months, he and his wife had listened to Jennifer's endless detailed descriptions of the house in her dream. The big white house with a porch and an attic. The only house where she could stay, where she could be happy again.

For nearly as long, he and Helen had tried to find that house, week after week, house after house. At first, it had been exciting, but now the whole business was starting to get to him. They'd looked at more than thirty houses, but none had been the right one for Jennifer.

He was beginning to wonder if the house existed at all. Still, it was wonderful to have his daughter around, talking and looking happy again. So he smiled as he turned back to her, trying to look interested.

"Where is it?" he asked. This time? he added silently.

"Well, it's a little far from here," Jennifer began, "out by Millbrook." Then her excitement took over. "But, Dad, it's amazing. It's got a huge attic, and a porch and library and apple trees and everything. Just like I dreamed."

Dreamed! Morgan thought, briefly tuning out his daughter again. Not dreamed, as in once or twice, but dreamed as in many dreams, night after night. Ever since the accident. And always the same dream, she says. About that house. A big house. White, with shutters. The friendly house, she calls it. But what if there is no friendly house? What if there is no dream? What if . . . ?

"So, will you call her now? Dad, are you listening?" Jennifer asked impatiently.

"Yes, dear, of course. Helen, could you come in here, please? Jennifer wants you," Morgan called out.

"Not Mom, Mrs. Jackson!" She rolled her eyes in frustration.

Mrs. Jackson was the real estate agent. She'd been showing them houses ever since they'd decided to move. But lately, Morgan thought, she seemed to be getting a little fed up with them.

Just last week she had said, "I've shown you every single big white house within a hundred kilometres, Mr. Ross. I don't know where to look next. Maybe you should take a break from house hunting for a while. Your wife seems very tired these days. Besides, you've got a lovely home already."

At that point, Morgan had stopped her.

"Not a home, Mrs. Jackson. Just a house. We must move. But, it has to be a house that's right for Jennifer."

"You said she's only eleven, Mr. Ross. I'm sure she'd get used to any house you bought." Impatience was creeping into Mrs. Jackson's voice.

"She's our only child, Mrs. Jackson." Morgan sighed. "You know how it is. We want her to be happy. That's all that ever mattered to us. So, if you'll just keep looking . . ."

And that's how they'd left it, with Mrs. Jackson promising to call as soon as she found something. But she hadn't sounded keen.

"What is it, Morgan?" Helen Ross asked, coming quietly into the kitchen.

It was true. She was looking worn out lately. And pale too. No sparkle left. No get-up-and-go. But when she saw Jennifer, she perked up a little.

"Oh, you're back, dear. Are you all right? You look . . ." she frowned thoughtfully, "different somehow."

"I'm so happy, Mom. And guess why? I found the friendly house at last. It's perfect."

"Do you really think so, Jennifer?"

"I know so. I went there three times. They're there, Mom. Like in the dream. I saw them."

"Jennifer wants us to call Mrs. Jackson, Helen," Morgan interrupted. "To see if the house is for sale. But I'm not so sure . . ."

"Do it, dear. We can't stay here. You know that. It's the only way."

"All right. I'll call from the den," Morgan said. "Tell me

again, Jennifer, exactly where this place is so I can pin it down for Mrs. Jackson."

Five minutes later, he was back in the kitchen, and he was smiling.

"She says it's listed."

Jennifer let out a whoop.

"It's been on the market for more than four years," Morgan continued. "But she says it's in such bad shape that she never dreamed of showing it to us."

"Don't worry, Dad. It's perfect. You'll see." Jennifer was so excited that she was flitting around the kitchen. "Should you start packing? When do we move? Let's go."

"Calm down, Jennifer," Morgan said. "You know you have to save your energy. We'll go and see the house tomorrow."

"Tomorrow?" Helen asked.

"Mrs. Jackson is busy today," Morgan explained. "She'll get the key tomorrow and meet us there in the evening. Around eight."

Millbrook was only a half-hour drive from Fenton, but Jennifer was so eager to show off the house that the Rosses had agreed to leave at six.

"So you can see it when it's still bright out," Jennifer had explained. "I'll show you the way when you get close."

"We could bring along some food and have a picnic first," Morgan had suggested hopefully. It had been a long time since Helen had wanted to do anything like that, and he wasn't sure what she'd say. But she had agreed, saying that it sounded like a great idea — until he'd mentioned the lake.

"We could spread out a blanket by the lake, like we used to, and . . ."

That's when Helen had gone pale again.

"Not the lake, Morgan," she had whispered hoarsely. "You know I can't go back there. Not since Jennifer . . ." Her voice trailed off into silence.

"No, of course not," Morgan had said quickly, reaching out to take his wife's hand. "I wasn't thinking."

Instead, he had proposed stopping along the way for hot dogs and ice cream, and Helen had said she'd like that a lot.

And that's exactly what they'd done. But it was still only seven-thirty when they turned off Highway 52 onto County Road 10.

Almost immediately, Jennifer spoke up from the back seat. "Keep a lookout, Dad. We're nearly there. See that gate up ahead on the left? Turn in there."

Morgan wheeled the car slowly down a long, tree-shaded lane.

"There it is. Isn't it beautiful?" Jennifer said softly, as the car pulled into a clearing.

"Well, it's certainly big enough," said her dad, shutting off the ignition.

"And it was white once," added her mother dubiously, as they got out of the car.

Jennifer skipped ahead of her parents.

"Come on, you two. Hurry up. Wait till you see inside," she called from the huge porch that ran around three sides of the house. Tall, shuttered windows opened onto it from each side of the front door.

"We have to wait for Mrs. Jackson," her dad called back. "She has the key."

"Oh, that's right. I forgot. You two need a key to get in," Jennifer giggled. Then she began to call out, "I'm here. I'm here," and drifted around the side of the house.

"All the patio furniture would fit on this porch," Morgan said, leading his wife up the steps after a walk around the property. "What do you think, Helen?"

"What do I think? I think that Jennifer will be happy here. Listen to her, Morgan. And did you see her when she got out of the car? She was positively glowing."

At that moment, Mrs. Jackson pulled into the lane and parked.

"Sorry I'm late," she called out as she grabbed her brief-case and hurried toward the porch.

"We're early," Morgan said. "And watch the steps. They need a little work."

"A little work? A lot of work, Mr. Ross. This whole place needs lots and lots of work. No one has lived here for years." Mrs. Jackson jumped back suddenly. "What's that? Did you hear that?"

"What?" Helen asked. "I didn't hear anything."

"Oh, I guess it's just me," Mrs. Jackson said. "Are you sure you want to see this place? It gives me the jitters. I can't imagine an eleven-year-old liking it. Did you finally bring Jennifer with you this time? I'd like to meet her."

I was right, Morgan thought. She *is* fed up with us.

Aloud, he simply said, "I told you she's uncomfortable with strangers. Now, can we go in and look around, please?"

Reluctantly, Mrs. Jackson pulled out a key, opened the door, and led the Rosses into the entrance hall.

Fifteen minutes later, she was edging back toward the hall, waiting impatiently for the Rosses to come downstairs.

Helen emerged from a bedroom and waved to her from the upstairs landing.

"I just wanted to take another look at the master bedroom," she said. "We're ready now."

Morgan joined her at the top of the stairs and, together, they slowly descended. They were smiling.

"We'll take it, Mrs. Jackson. When can we move in?" Morgan said.

Mrs. Jackson's cheeks turned bright red. "But you haven't even asked the price yet. Mind you, that won't be a problem. It's very low — less than half what your own house is worth. But . . ." she hesitated.

"But what?" Helen asked.

"Look, Mrs. Ross. I'd be lying if I said I didn't want this sale. I've spent more time with you people than I have with any other clients. I mean, we've been looking for nearly nine months. But I really don't think you should buy this house. And not just because of the state it's in."

"Why not?" asked Morgan.

Mrs. Jackson hesitated again, then continued. "This afternoon, when I stopped to pick up the key from the local real estate agent, he . . ." she paused.

"Go on," Helen said.

"Well, he told me something about the house." Mrs. Jackson lowered her voice. "Of course, I don't believe stuff like this myself, but he said some people think it's haunted."

"Really?" Helen said. "Tell us more."

Mrs. Jackson looked around nervously. Speaking nearly in a whisper, she continued, "Well, apparently a family used to live here, the Moranos. They had two children — a girl, eleven, and a boy, thirteen. Five years ago, there was a terrible crash on Highway 52. Their car went off the bridge. Mr. and Mrs. Morano were saved, but not the children. They drowned. The Moranos left the house about a month later. The children had loved it out here in the country, but the house was too empty without them. It held too many memories for the parents. They just had to move."

Helen's eyes grew misty. "I know just how they felt." Then she added, "How sad. It's always terrible to lose a child."

"But," Mrs. Jackson said, speaking quickly now, "people say the children aren't really lost, gone, whatever. Some say they're still here. They say they've seen them. The two of them. Playing out in the yard, and moving past the windows late at night. Some people say they've even heard them singing. Laughing too. And just last week, the agent says he saw three shapes at the window, not just two. Even he is starting to believe the stories."

Mrs. Jackson's cheeks were burning now. "So do you see why you probably shouldn't buy this house? Besides, your daughter will hate it. She'll be scared to death of the place."

Mrs. Jackson was opening the door now, ushering the Rosses onto the porch. Then she froze. "Did you hear that?" she croaked.

"Hear what?" Morgan asked, stepping outside.

"I thought I heard someone laughing."

"Where? Inside?" he asked.

"No, over there," Mrs. Jackson said, pointing toward a small, neglected orchard. "But there's nothing there."

Helen and Morgan looked toward the orchard. In the glow of the sunset, they could just make out the misty shapes of three children, two girls and a boy. They were darting in and out among the old apple trees as if they were playing tag.

Helen and Morgan looked back at each other and smiled.

"We'll take the house, Mrs. Jackson," they said together.

"But your daughter . . . You said she didn't want all the other houses. I'm sure she'll hate this one."

"I don't think so," Morgan said. "I think she'll find it a very friendly house, don't you, Helen?"

"I know she will," Helen said. "She'll probably say it's a dream come true."

A BOY'S BEST FRIEND

Only one thing got Marshall through the miserable weeks after his dog, Fred, was hit by a car and killed. That was thoughts of summer camp.

Whenever memories of Fred started to get to him, he'd check the calendar over his desk and count off the days till camp was due to start.

Finally, it was the night before he was to leave for another magical summer at White Pine. Marshall picked up the picture of himself and Fred that he kept on his bedside table.

"G'night, buddy," he said, as he did every night. Then he tucked it into the side pocket of his bag, right next to his three new Gordon Korman books.

"White Pine, here I come," he thought as he snuggled under the covers. For the first time in months, he felt really and truly happy.

But his happiness was short-lived. It lasted through the two-hour bus ride to the camp and through the silly greetings the counsellors invented for the campers. But it ended abruptly the moment Marshall opened the door of his cabin.

There, on bed number six — right beside his — sat

Zack Vincent, perpetrator of countless Zack Attacks. That's what the other campers called the things Zack did to his victims. Most of them had suffered through at least one Zack Attack.

Zack worked hard at keeping his reputation as the camp bully. Somehow, he must have sensed that Marshall was ripe for the picking. He launched his first attack right away.

"Well, well, well, if it isn't Sheriff. Or is it Deputy? No, wait. Now I've got it. It's Marrrrr-shull."

The way Zack said it, Marshall almost wished his name were Dumbo. He walked slowly over to his bed, trying to ignore the fact that the other boys were watching, waiting to see what he'd do. Tyler, a friend from last year, was the only one who might stick up for him.

"Hey, Marrrrr-shull. Where's your badge? You going to arrest me, Marrrrr-shull?"

Somebody should, Marshall thought, but he said nothing. He simply went about unpacking his bag, wishing with all his heart that his mother's expression, Ignore it — it'll go away, were true.

But Zack wasn't going anywhere, and he was impossible to ignore. In the next few days, he hid Marshall's runners, short-sheeted his bed, flipped a garter snake over the top of the stall while Marshall showered, and poured water into his bed while he slept.

Marshall woke embarrassed, convinced he'd wet his bed. It was only later, when he overheard Zack bragging about it, that he realized what had happened. He was living a nightmare and there was no end in sight.

That night after dinner, Marshall asked to be excused from campfire. It was the first time he'd done it, so the counsellors gave him permission.

Thankful for some time to himself, Marshall got ready for bed and scrunched down under the covers with his flashlight, a book and his picture of Fred. He'd been using it as a bookmark all through camp. That way he could sneak a peek at it as often as he wanted.

Tyler had asked about Fred. Tyler had a dog, too — Bowser. The previous summer, he and Marshall had spent a lot of time swapping dog stories.

This summer, though, there was no more dog talk. Tyler didn't want to hurt Marshall's feelings by going on about how great Bowser was. And Marshall didn't dare talk about Fred for fear he'd start to cry. Zack would have a field day if he ever caught Marshall bawling like a baby.

Fred and Zack. The two had become woven together in Marshall's mind. The more Zack tormented him, the more he longed to have Fred back.

He stared at Fred's picture, wishing he could make him materialize. Then it wouldn't matter what Zack did to him.

Fred and Zack. Zack and Fred. Marshall forced his eyes to stay open just long enough so he could switch off his flashlight and stuff his book — and bookmark — under his pillow. Then he curled up on his side, his back to Zack's bed, and fell asleep.

It was still dark when Marshall woke up, covered in sweat and shaking like Jell-O. The nightmare again. The one that had haunted him ever since camp started.

In it, Marshall stood over Zack, watching him choke

on a peanut butter sandwich. Fred was there too, yapping and biting at Zack's ankles. As Zack writhed helplessly on the cabin floor, Marshall felt himself starting to laugh — a loud, gloating cackle that turned his blood to ice. As Zack gasped and held out his hands for help, Marshall turned his back and walked toward the door.

But the door was covered by an enormous piece of paper. On it, scrawled in huge letters, was a Chinese proverb: *He who seeks revenge should dig two graves.* Marshall had seen it before — in English class when his teacher used it to introduce a story about a man trying to get even with a friend who had betrayed him.

The paper swayed, blocking Marshall's exit. Still laughing horribly, he tore through it and pushed his way outside.

For a moment, he felt himself floating. In the dark below were two freshly dug graves. Zack's lifeless body lay in one. Then he started to fall.

That's when he always woke up. Every night. Right on cue. His arms flailing, struggling to stop himself from falling into the second grave.

The cabin was quiet, except for the rhythmic buzz of Tyler's snoring. As his eyes adjusted to the darkness, Marshall could just make out Zack, lying on his side, facing him. Zack was sound asleep, a smile creasing the corners of his mouth.

He's probably dreaming about what he's going to do to me tomorrow, Marshall thought. I wish he'd disappear. And, most of all, I wish you were here, Fred. I'd sic you on that creep. You'd teach him a thing or two. Geez, I miss you, little buddy.

Marshall eventually fell asleep again, his eyes moist with secret, silent tears.

Things got worse the next morning. His tossing and turning during the night must have knocked his book to the floor. He woke up to find Zack waving Fred's picture in front of his eyes.

"So, who's this, Marrrrr-shull? Your girlfriend? Hey, guys, Marshall's girlfriend is a real dog." Zack laughed mockingly. Some of the other kids joined in weakly.

"Give it back," Marshall said, trying to get up. Zack leaned over and shoved the picture into Marshall's face.

"Give it back," Marshall mumbled.

Zack didn't budge. Suddenly Marshall pulled back both legs and kicked with all his might. Zack tumbled to the floor. Marshall followed, in a tangle of sheets and blankets.

"Give it to me, Zack. Right now. It's mine." Zack scrambled to his feet and moved to the other side of the bunk.

"Marshall's girlfriend's a dog. Marshall's girlfriend's a dog," he taunted.

Marshall struggled to stand up. As he got to his feet, he tripped on the sheet and fell across Zack's bed. Desperately, he grabbed for the picture.

"You want it?" Zack jeered. "Here, have it." He ripped the photo apart, crumpled the pieces, and tossed them at Marshall. Then he turned and headed for the door.

Marshall picked up the pieces and stood up. Fighting back tears, he yelled, "You'll be sorry for this, Zack. You wait. You're nothing but a bully. That's all. A scummy, scuzzy, brainless bully!"

Someone gasped. Then there was dead silence in the

51

cabin. Shocked, everyone was quiet, including Marshall.

Slowly, Zack swung around and glared at him. Then, as if deciding that he'd done enough damage, he turned and strolled out the door.

Marshall tried to salvage the photograph. He spread out the pieces on his bunk, hoping he'd be able to tape them back together. It was no use. Fred's face was torn right down the middle and white cracks showed where Zack had crumpled the pieces. The picture was ruined. Fred was gone, and now so was his photograph.

Thoughts of Fred and what Zack had done weighed heavily on Marshall as he trudged to the dining hall for breakfast. He didn't dare line up at the steam table for scrambled eggs and sausages. That was a favourite place for Zack to carry out a sneak attack on his victims.

Instead, he went directly to his cabin's table where there was a supply of toast, cereal and juice. Before he sat down beside Tyler, he checked his chair to make sure Zack hadn't painted it with jam.

As if reading his mind, Tyler said, "Don't worry. He's not here."

"Where is he?" Marshall asked.

"Gone to have a shower," Tyler said, breaking into a grin. "He never made it to breakfast. He tripped and fell into the worst mud puddle around. Even some of the counsellors laughed."

"You're kidding."

"Nope. It was great. You should have been there."

Marshall was there the next time Zack tripped, on the way to lunch. And he was there when Zack stumbled on the way to the dock, too. He had his bathing suit on and skinned his knees badly.

Then he collapsed on the way to the campfire, letting out an agonized yell as he tumbled to his battered knees again. This time, Marshall actually winced in sympathy.

That night, Zack went to bed without tormenting anyone, not even Marshall. Marshall fell asleep smiling. At last Zack was getting exactly what he deserved.

For the first time since camp started, Marshall slept peacefully and woke feeling refreshed. Zack, however, woke up grumpy as a grizzly bear, complaining that he'd nearly frozen to death.

". . . and whoever kept pulling off the covers better watch out," he threatened. "When I catch him, he'll wish he'd never been born." He glared straight at Marshall as he said this. Then he snatched his blankets off the floor and began to make his bed.

Marshall made his own bed quickly, anxious to get as far from Zack as possible. In a mood like that, there was no telling what he might do.

Mind you, Marshall thought, losing your blankets like that could be really irritating, especially on a cool night. He remembered how Fred sometimes used to pull off his covers. He hated waking up chilled to the bone.

That day, strange things continued to happen to Zack. In the morning, he fell backwards off the dock, claiming a horsefly had taken a huge chunk out of his ankle. But when the waterfront director offered him AfterBite to rub on the spot, Zack could find no sign of swelling or redness anywhere.

At dinner — a wiener roast around the fire — Zack claimed that someone snatched his hot dog. Even though he'd cooked it and drowned it in ketchup himself, he was convinced that someone had tied a string to it and yanked it away.

When the counsellors told him to lighten up, he flew into a rage and stormed off. He was lying in bed, his face pressed into his pillow, when the others returned.

The next morning, the cabin woke to more of Zack's ranting.

"If I catch that dog, I'll stuff him in a sack with a big rock and heave him into the lake."

"What dog?" Tyler asked.

"The one that yapped outside all night."

"I didn't hear any dog," Tyler said. "Did you guys?"

The others, Marshall included, shook their heads, mystified.

"What do you mean, you didn't hear it? Are you deaf? Yap, yap, yap — all night long. I'm going to set a wolf trap out there tonight."

Zack's talk of a yapping dog reminded Marshall of Fred. Fred used to do that sometimes — yap, yap, yap, until he got what he wanted. Wait a minute, Marshall thought. Fred used to pull the covers off my bed, too. And snatch food at barbecues. That was one of his favourite tricks.

Suddenly, there was a loud crash followed by a scream. Zack lay sprawled at the bottom of the cabin steps. He was crying.

Giggles rippled through the cabin. The mighty Attacker was blubbering like a baby.

Someone called out "Wacko Zacko" and the giggles turned to hoots of mocking laughter. Everyone was laughing. Everyone except Tyler, who never laughed at other people's troubles — and Marshall.

Marshall wasn't laughing because he'd just added another item to his mental list. Fred was always underfoot. It seemed like someone was forever tripping over him. This is impossible, Marshall thought. It can't be. Fred is . . .

Zack screamed again. Tyler and Raj, who were trying to help him up, jumped back.

"My leg," Zack moaned, collapsing against Tyler. "I can't stand up. Get help. I think it's broken."

Marshall ran and collected two counsellors who used a firefighter's lift to carry Zack to the infirmary. Marshall and the others trailed behind, then hung around outside waiting for word on Zack's injury.

Finally, the nurse emerged to announce that Zack's leg wasn't broken, but it was badly sprained.

"He'll be spending the next couple of days in the infirmary," he said.

The rest of the day was great. With Zack safely out of commission, everyone relaxed. Everyone except Marshall. He struggled to come up with an explanation for what was happening. Every time, he got the same impossible answer — Fred.

Later that evening, when the other kids were changing into their bathing suits for a midnight swim, Marshall slipped off to the infirmary. Quietly, he skulked around it. Then, he stood statue-still under the window and listened intently. He saw and heard nothing unusual.

Finally, he crouched in the darkness and whispered, "Fred, Fred. Here boy. C'mere, boy." Nothing. Nevertheless, he went on.

"Listen to me, boy. I think you're out there. If you are, thanks. You really came through. But, Fred, it's over now, okay? I can't stand to see Zack feeling like I did. Give the guy a break, Fred. He's got no friends. I'm okay now, fella. Really, I am."

As Marshall stood up to leave, he stepped on a stick. It snapped with a loud crack.

"Who's there?" Zack called out sharply. Fear filled his voice. "Is that you, dog?"

Marshall wavered. Should I answer — or just get out of here? He sounds really scared.

"It's me, Zack. Marshall."

"What are you doing out there?" Some of the bravado was returning to Zack's voice.

"Oh . . . I just came by to say good night."

"Yeah?" Zack sounded surprised.

"Yeah," Marshall said, pushing open the door. In the glow of a night light, Marshall could just see Zack's head poking out from under the covers.

"Shhh," Zack whispered. "The nurse might not be asleep yet. He just finished putting ice on my ankle a while ago."

"How's the leg?" Marshall whispered back.

"It hurts."

"Sorry."

"So am I."

Marshall couldn't believe his ears. "What did you say?" he asked.

"I said, So am I." Zack looked like he was bracing for Marshall to say something mean.

Marshall stared. Then he said softly, "It's okay."

Zack let out his breath and his face softened. "Thanks," he said.

"No problem. See you in the morning?"

"Sure."

Marshall tiptoed back to his cabin and slipped into bed. By the time the others got back from their swim, he was sound asleep. He dreamed that Fred was curled up at the foot of his bed.

After breakfast, Marshall returned to the infirmary. Zack was sitting up, eating breakfast. "How's the leg?" Marshall asked.

"Much better, thanks."

"Great," said Marshall. "Does it still hurt?"

"Not too much. I think the nurse must have put a heating pad on it in the night. I remember waking up and thinking how good it felt to have something soft and warm tucked around my ankle."

Marshall looked at the foot of the bed, then at Zack. Smiling, he said, "Yeah, I know just what you mean."

ROBBER'S REWARD

The day started like any other. Julie's mother, a lab technician, left for the hospital around seven-thirty. Her dad wasn't home yet from another night of driving his cab. Julie and her sister fought over the bathroom and, as usual, she lost.

Finally, Ruby headed off to school — her classes started at eight-thirty — and Julie had a few minutes to herself. She flicked on the TV and began to crunch her way through a bowl of corn flakes.

The news was on — not exactly prime time viewing. Her thoughts wandered to the science fair topic she'd decided on last night. For once, she'd picked something she was really interested in.

She wanted to know why the shower curtain moved in and wrapped itself around her when she turned on the water. So did Ruby. She always screamed "Soap scum attack!" when it happened to her.

Her mom said a lot of science could be learned by answering this question, and she was pretty smart about math and science. She wasn't so sure about her teacher, though. And he was the one who needed to give the green light to her topic this morning.

". . . and police are still at the scene of the bank break-in at Fifth and Fraser . . ."

Fifth and Fraser! That was just three blocks away. Julie passed that corner every morning on the way to school. She suddenly tuned in to the newscaster's words.

"Reports are still sketchy, but it looks as if the alarm may have interrupted a burglary in progress. The first officers on the scene found a man, believed to be one of the suspects, dead in front of the vault. Detective Coleman of 22 Division refused to speculate about how the man died. He would say only that it's clear the dead man had not been alone in the bank. Police are asking people to avoid that intersection until . . ."

Julie jumped up from the table. She switched off the TV, dumped her bowl in the sink and tore into her bedroom. She grabbed her backpack, stopped off at the bathroom to give her teeth a two-second brush, and dashed out of the apartment.

A large crowd was gathered in front of the bank when Julie got there. She jostled her way through the people until she was stopped by a thick, yellow plastic ribbon that warned: Police Line — Do Not Cross.

Julie was fascinated. An ambulance, its red lights flashing, was parked near the door of the bank. Police cars and equipment vans emblazoned with the logos of the city's TV stations were everywhere. Reporters and camera crews were scurrying about, and police officers were questioning people on the street and controlling the parade of individuals moving into and out of the bank.

Through the bank's double entrance doors, Julie could

just make out a small circle of people hovering over something on the floor. That must be where the body is, she thought. They never move it until they've looked for all the evidence. She knew that. It always happened that way on TV.

Suddenly, police officers moved to the doors and held them open as two uniformed paramedics began to walk slowly forward. Julie realized what was happening. They were bringing out the body.

The crowd grew silent as the paramedics emerged and loaded the stretcher carefully into the ambulance. Julie stared. It was exciting, but it bothered her, too. Someone had died. Somebody's brother, husband or even father.

"Husband *and* father," she heard a voice say.

"Huh?" Julie swung around to see who'd spoken. No one was paying any attention to her. She turned back, feeling foolish. For a second, she could have sworn someone had read her mind.

"I did. Weird, isn't it?" she heard the voice again.

Julie spun around. Again, no one was even looking her way. The crowd was thinning now. The person closest to her — an older woman — was several steps away. But the voice, a low, throaty whisper, had sounded as if it were right at her ear. It was a man's voice.

"I'm right here, kid."

Julie shivered. This is spooky, she thought. She'd heard voices before, at summer camp. But that had been Rachel McKenzie up to her usual tricks. She loved to wait until someone was asleep, then whisper weird noises in her ear. Rachel wasn't anywhere around. In fact, right now, Rachel was probably at school, waiting for the bell to ring.

And that's where I should be, too, Julie decided. Her mother always said her imagination worked overtime. Too much television, she'd say. It does things to your brain. Julie backed away from the yellow tape and started to jog along Fifth Street toward the school.

"Slow down, kid. I'm new at this."

The voice was following her. She was sure of it now. Terrified, Julie began to run.

"Wait. This is using up too much energy."

Julie felt a tugging at her back. She stopped and whipped around. Nothing. There was nothing there. She was petrified, too scared to move. She stood rooted to the spot, her knees knocking and her stomach churning.

"Sorry, kid. But it worked. You stopped. Now will you listen to me, please?"

Julie detected a note of desperation in the voice. Stay or go? School was just two blocks away. Go to school. You'll be safe there, she thought.

"Maybe not. I haven't gone through any walls yet, but I'm willing to try. Besides, there's always a window."

"All right, all right," Julie muttered, trying not to move her lips. She looked around to see if anyone had heard. She didn't want any of the other kids to see her talking to herself. Luckily, the coast was clear, for the moment.

She ducked up an alley and stammered, "Who . . . whoever or . . . whatever you are . . . what do you want from me?"

I can't believe I'm doing this, she thought. I'm talking to it, whatever it is. Am I crazy or what?

"You're not crazy. But I was . . . and now I'm dead. And I shouldn't be, you know."

Suddenly, the metal lid from a battered garbage can clattered to the pavement next to her. Julie jumped as the sound echoed up and down the alley. Then she heard rustling in the can. She stood perfectly still. More rustling, and some scratching. Julie stopped breathing. More scratching. Her imagination shifted into high gear. What sort of spectre was about to materialize?

When a scraggly tabby cat poked its face over the top of the can and blinked at her, Julie let out a long, slow sigh of relief. The cat jumped lightly to the ground and ran off. Julie was tempted to follow. Instead, she looked around one more time to make sure she was alone.

Alone? That's funny, she thought. I wish I really were alone. Then it hit her. Whatever it was, it had figured out what she was thinking. She hated the idea of someone being in her head like that. But it would take care of the problem of getting caught talking out loud to empty space.

What are you? Julie thought. What do you want from me? Silence. She concentrated harder. What do you want? Not a sound. It's gone! Or I'm sane again, she thought. This might be her chance to escape. She turned to leave.

"Stop, please. Don't go." The voice was coming from her right, over by the wall.

Julie's fear returned. She shut her eyes and concentrated even harder. What do you want?

"Please, say something. Say you'll help."

"Why do I have to say something?" Julie whispered. "You know what I'm thinking."

"I can't seem to do that anymore. It started when they loaded me onto the stretcher. I knew what the cops were thinking. Then, when they wheeled me out to the ambulance, all sorts of thoughts came flooding in. All those people. It was rough. That crowd was pretty hostile. Some ugly thoughts out there. Except for you. You thought about my family."

The voice paused briefly. Julie thought she heard a sob. Then the voice went on.

"That's why I picked you. But I can't read your mind anymore. In fact, I don't know how much time I have left. Everything is starting to feel different. Will you help me?"

The impact of what she'd just heard hit Julie in the stomach like a baseball bat.

"You're the . . ." Julie gulped. "You're the . . . uh . . . man at the bank?"

"The dead guy. Yeah."

Julie gasped. "Ok-k-kay," she sputtered, trying to sound calm. "I have to go now. I'm going to get it. I'm really late for school."

"Don't go. Not yet. I have to set the record straight. You've got to help me do that. Please, for my boy's sake," the voice pleaded.

"But why should I help you? You're a . . ."

"A thief? A crook? Say it, kid. It's true. I know it was really stupid, but I needed the money and . . . well . . . I let my friend talk me into it. But it was the first time. Really. You've got to believe me."

"I don't know what to believe anymore."

"I know how you feel. But listen, please. First, my name's Jim. Jim Robertson. And you're . . . ?"

"Julie." Julie hesitated. Last names made it easier for

someone to find you. Then she realized how ridiculous that thought was. This thing, this spirit, this ghost could probably find her anywhere, anytime.

"Sharma," she added. "Julie Sharma." *There. I've done it. I just introduced myself to a ghost.*

"Pleased to meet you, Julie. I'm telling the truth. It really was the first time. It's no excuse, I know, but things were bad. I'd lost my job. My wife and son had left, the rent was overdue and the landlord was threatening to throw me out of the apartment.

"So Nick — my best friend, Nick — came up with this plan. Nothing to it, the lying scumbag said. He used to work at the bank as a security guard. I know the layout, he said. No one'll get hurt. Ha. What a joke!"

"What went wrong?" Julie was surprised to find herself interested.

"Nothing, at first. Everything went like clockwork until . . ."

Suddenly, everything became clear to Julie. "Until he tricked you," she blurted. "When he didn't need you anymore, he killed you, right, and took the money for himself?"

"That's right. And now Nick'll get away with the money — and with murder. My murder. And the truth will never come out. Not that it's so pretty. But, if the cops get Nick, maybe my ex-wife will understand a little better. Maybe she'll be able to explain things to the boy when he's bigger. I'm not all bad, you know." The voice trailed off at that point.

Julie had a minute to think. *I'm already in big trouble. School started half an hour ago. And not even the most gullible teacher will believe this story.* Aloud she said,

"Okay, what can I do?"

"Thanks, kid," the voice sounded relieved, but tired. It seemed to be growing fainter. "Here's what you can do. There's this crime tip number . . ."

"I know. I hear it on TV all the time. It's 577 —"

"Good, you know it. We'll go to that pay phone over there. If you dial the number for me, I'll tell them what happened at the bank. They won't know it's me. They'll just think I'm a sleazeball turning in a friend. And they'll be right, won't they? I'll give them my good old friend, Nick."

"That's it? That's all you want?"

"That's it. If I could do it myself, I would."

"Okay, let's go then," Julie said, reaching into her pocket for some change.

Julie dialed the number and kept the receiver to her ear as a deep voice answered, "Constable Tremblay. Thank you for calling Crime Tips."

Julie could almost feel Jim leaning beside her. Shivers rippled down her spine.

"Hello," Jim said, "I know what happened at . . ."

"Hello?" Tremblay repeated. "Is anybody there?"

Julie held out the phone a little farther, trying to figure out how to make it easier for Jim to speak into the receiver.

"I'm here," Jim spoke up. "A man named Nick . . ."

"Is anyone there? Hello?" Tremblay said loudly.

"He can't hear me, kid! He can't hear me," Jim said, panic in his voice. "What'll I do? Can you hear me? Am I gone?"

"I hear you," Julie said, covering the mouthpiece. "But maybe I'm the only one who can."

"Oh no," Jim moaned.

Julie looked at the receiver in her hand. She swallowed hard and put the phone back to her ear.

"I'm sorry," she began nervously. "I dropped the phone."

Shakily, she told the officer what she'd learned. Jim helped, whispering the answers to the officer's questions. Julie even managed to work in information about where Nick planned to hide the money — in a locker at the bus terminal.

She could almost feel Jim nodding enthusiastically when she added that if the police staked out the terminal, they could probably catch Nick red-handed when he went to pick up the money.

But when Tremblay asked how to get the reward to her if the tip led to an arrest, Julie panicked. She covered the mouthpiece.

"Go for it," Jim whispered hoarsely. "You earned it. You don't have to give your name. They'll work out something with you."

Julie was tempted. Crime Tips paid $1,000 if an arrest was made. But somehow it didn't seem right to take it, and she wasn't sure why.

"Just a minute, please," she said, and covered the mouthpiece again.

"Jim, what's your wife's name?"

"Maria," Jim answered faintly. "Maria Lopez. She went back to her own name."

"And her address?"

"1394 Merton, Apartment 1B. Why?"

Julie spoke quickly into the phone, "The reward goes to Maria Lopez, 1394 Merton, Apartment 1B. Goodbye."

She hung up and slumped against the wall of the phone booth. Her knees were trembling.

Weakly, Jim said, "Thanks, Julie. You're something else. Your folks must be really proud of you."

At the mention of her folks, Julie panicked and pushed her way out of the phone booth.

"Well, they won't be if the school called already to find out why I'm not there. I've really gotta go."

"So do I, kid. I think my time's nearly up."

"Well . . . good luck."

What an unbelievably dumb thing to say! Julie thought. Then she started to run. There'd be time to think later, after she got to school.

By the time she reached her homeroom, Julie had decided to go with a version of the truth. As Mr. Falconi glared at her, she explained that she'd stopped to watch what was going on at the bank and lost track of time.

Mr. Falconi lectured her on the evils of lateness, then levelled a parting shot. "And I suppose you also lost track of your science fair topic."

"No, I've got that."

"Well, what is it? How to investigate bank robberies in three easy lessons?" Some of the kids giggled.

"No . . . it's to find out why the curtain moves in toward you when you turn on the shower." That started even more giggles.

"What did you say? You're on thin ice already, Ms. Sharma. This is no time for joking."

"I'm not joking, Mr. Falconi."

Julie heard a faint whisper in her ear. "The window, kid. Look. Hurry."

Oh no, Julie thought. I can't take this.

"Hurry, kid. I haven't got much more time."

Julie looked at the open windows that lined the wall of the classroom. Shapeless blue drapes hung limply over them. Suddenly, a single pair of drapes swayed slightly, then pressed against the open window, as if they were being sucked outside.

"There, like that," Julie pointed at the window.

"Yeah, why does that happen?" Rachel McKenzie yelled.

"I guess Julie will find out and tell us," Mr. Falconi said. "I wonder why it happened at only one window."

"Probably just a fluke breeze," Julie offered, watching the drapes fall back into place. Once again, like the air outside, they were perfectly still. Thanks, Jim, she thought. Goodbye.

RESCUE BY NUMBERS

I can't believe I'm doing this, Pete thought, as he peeled back the small plastic lid labelled Number 1. The oily smell hit him instantly. At least they haven't dried out, he noted. He dipped the fine-tipped brush into the inky blue paint and stirred gently. Carefully, he wiped the excess on the edge of the little pot, then held the brush poised over the faint blue maze covering the white canvas.

"Looks like you got your way after all, Grandma," he muttered ruefully, steadying his hand.

He lowered the brush and filled in the first irregular shape marked with a tiny blue 1. As the colour oozed past the outline, he realized he'd have to be careful about the amount of paint he applied. Doing this picture was going to take a long time. But time is something I've got plenty of now, right? he told himself, as he dabbed paint over another 1.

"And how did you spend your summer holidays, Pete?" he imagined Ms Tompkins asking when he got back to school.

"Oh, doing a paint-by-numbers kit," he pictured himself answering. "It was loads of fun."

Pete grimaced, feeling sorry for himself. The pain in his

right calf was down to a dull throb, not nearly as bad as it had been yesterday, but it still hurt a lot. He wished he could take back those few moments yesterday afternoon.

If only he'd been content to stay inside the lodge's roped-off swimming area. If only he hadn't tried to show off by slipping under the rope and swimming out to the point. If only he'd paid attention as he climbed onto the slippery, moss-covered rocks, rather than trying to wave to the kids who'd stayed safely behind.

If only . . . maybe he wouldn't have slipped and opened up a sixteen-stitch gash in his leg. And maybe he'd be where he wanted to be today — white-water rafting.

His parents had offered to stay behind to keep him company, but he knew how much they'd been looking forward to the rafting. He'd been dreaming about it himself for the last two months.

So he told them he'd be just fine in the cabin on his own and persuaded them to go without him.

Before they left, they'd stocked the fridge with plenty of pop and sandwiches.

"Just in case it hurts too much to go over to the cafeteria," Mom explained, adding two new bags of corn chips to the already impressive stash of junk food on the old wooden sideboard.

"And Mr. Kramer is just a call away," Dad added, pointing to the phone. "We checked with him earlier and he says he'll be happy to keep an eye on you."

"Dad, his office is right there," Pete said, pointing out the window. "Mr. Kramer could hear me from here even if I just whispered, okay?"

But, to humour Dad, he'd promised to phone the lodge owner. "Now get going. There's the van. I'll be fine. I'm not a baby anymore. Go."

Finally, they left. Pete waved from the doorway until the lodge van was out of sight.

Back inside the cabin, though, he couldn't settle. He felt restless. He tried reading for a while, but an old Hardy Boys adventure failed to grab him. He turned on the radio, but a man talking about home improvements was the only static-free show he could find.

It was when he reached over to turn off the radio that he spotted the box on the floor. His grandmother had handed it to him three days earlier, just as he and his folks were leaving for their vacation.

"Grandpa wants you to have this," she had said, holding it out. "It was his. He never got to work on it."

She'd paused for a moment, a faraway look in her eyes, then added, "The picture on top seems to have gone missing, but everything else is fine. Your grandpa loved doing these, you know. That's how he made the two pictures in my bedroom. Last night when I was looking at them, he told me you'd need this on your trip. Have fun with it and bring me back a beautiful picture. I'll put it on my wall, too."

"But I'll be way too busy, Grandma," Pete had protested lamely. "Maybe you should keep it here so it won't get wrecked."

But Grandma had insisted, and he had reluctantly packed the kit. He hadn't wanted to hurt her feelings by coming right out and saying that there was no way he was going to spend his holiday doing a paint-by-numbers.

Besides, since Grandma had come to live with them last year, he'd learned that there was no point in trying to make sense of some of the things she said about Grandpa. It worried him that she thought a dead person talked to her every now and then, but he knew how lonely she was. As Dad said, it was probably just her way of dealing with not having Grandpa with her anymore.

"The bonds of love are pretty strong," Dad had tried to explain, "especially after forty years. She still feels them, that's all."

Pete paused and looked at the canvas. He was surprised to see how many tiny spaces he'd filled in while his mind had been wandering.

Clearly, the dark blue made up much of the top section. Probably sky, he thought. Suddenly, he wished he had the picture that had originally been stuck to the top of the box. It would be nice to know what he was painting a picture of.

He decided to switch to another colour. He was running out of places where he could rest his hand without touching a sticky blue spot. Obviously, oil paint took longer to dry than watercolours.

Maybe I should let it dry a bit and come back to it later, he thought as he snapped the lid back on the Number 1 container. But as he wiped the brush on a paper towel, he was surprised to realize that he wanted to keep painting.

He studied the bottom of the canvas carefully and decided to open the green pot labelled Number 8. There were lots of little 8 shapes scattered across the lower third of the picture, and he could lean his hand on the table as he filled them in.

This time, Pete barely tapped the tip of the brush into the paint. This way, the brush kept its fine point and picked up just enough green to fill in a shape without oozing over the edge.

It crossed his mind that he was actually getting the knack of painting by numbers. The thought left him feeling both pleased and a little foolish — pleased because he was getting better at it, but foolish that he was getting any pleasure at all out of something so ridiculous. Try as he might, though, he couldn't talk himself out of doing it.

He'd been working for quite a while when the sound of heavy boots trudging up the front steps broke his concentration. He looked up to see Mr. Kramer poised to knock on the screen door.

"Hi, Mr. Kramer," he called and pushed himself away from the table. Only then did he realize how much his leg still hurt. He'd forgotten all about it while he was painting, but as he scrambled to stand up, a stab of pain shot up his thigh.

Despite the pain, he was determined to head off Mr. Kramer at the doorway. The last thing he wanted was for anyone to see what he was doing.

"Still hurting, eh?" Mr. Kramer commented as Pete limped toward him.

"Sort of," Pete answered, "but mostly when I walk on it, that's all."

"Well, your folks asked me to check on you, so here I am. How about I help you over to the dining hall for lunch?"

Lunch. Pete couldn't believe that it was lunchtime already.

"Or maybe you'd like to come sit on the dock and do some fishing? What do you say to that?"

"Thanks a lot, Mr. Kramer, but I'm fine, really. I've got plenty to eat and stuff to read. I think I'd just as soon hang around here for now. Maybe I'll come down later this afternoon, okay?"

"Up to you, son. Just give me a shout if you need a hand."

"I will, I promise. Thanks again."

Pete watched as Mr. Kramer walked briskly back to his office. The noonday sun was dancing on the lake and many of the guests had retreated to the picnic tables tucked under the trees.

Why am I in here? Pete wondered. The answer that popped into his head left him feeling unsettled. Because I have to do the picture, he found himself thinking as he shuffled back to the table.

This thought bothered him and, when he looked down at the painting, he was even more disturbed. He hadn't realized how much of it was finished. He had only vague memories of opening the lighter green, rusty brown, black and pale blue pots, and didn't remember at all using the creamy white to top off what was obviously foaming, tumbling water.

Parts of the picture were actually starting to take shape, and they looked good. All the little sections were starting to fit together like the pieces of a puzzle. The effect was pretty impressive. But it was disturbing, too. The empty spaces seemed to cry out for the missing colours that would define them as trees, flowers, water, clouds or sky.

Pete was hungry — and tired. He realized his leg was throbbing. He wanted to take a break. But something stopped him. Something told him he had to finish the painting as quickly as possible.

His hand shook a little as he dipped the brush into a dark grey Number 12. Wondering what this colour would reveal, he began to apply it methodically to the many small 12s on the left side of the picture. Rocks, he thought. They're rocks, poking out of the water.

"Hey, I get it," he announced. "It's rapids." Feeling pleased with himself, he began to work more quickly, eager to make sense of the unpainted sections along the shore of the racing river that was taking shape before him.

The faster Pete worked, the quicker the paint seemed to dry. He no longer had to worry about smearing it the way he had in the morning. And, once again, he was barely aware of the mechanics of what he was doing.

What he was noticing, however, in sharper and sharper detail, was how slivers of brown were actually parts of tall pines, dots of black were bark markings on spindly birches, and wedges of dark grey were weathered cedar shingles on a cabin tucked into the hillside. He had the growing sense that he was no longer filling in numbers but actually painting a picture.

For the first time, he checked his watch. Five o'clock. The day had disappeared. He wondered vaguely why his parents weren't back yet. Then he became aware that his head was aching. His throat was dry, too, and his fingers felt cramped and twisted. And in the background was the pulsing pain in his leg.

Pete began to worry about the gash. Maybe it was infected. The doctor had warned him to watch out for that. Maybe his throat was dry and his head ached because he had a fever, a fever caused by poison spreading through his body from the wound.

Then it hit him. There was a fever burning in him all right, but it wasn't caused by infection. It was a fever of fear. With a shiver, Pete suddenly realized that he was afraid of what lay in front of him. He was afraid of the picture.

His hand began to shake and his eyes blurred. He put down the brush and rubbed his eyes. Then he stared at the painting again. There was something hauntingly familiar about it.

He tried to focus on the scene. Slowly it dawned on him that he had seen this place before. But where? And what did it matter if he had?

Crazy as it seemed, he felt sure that it did matter. He had to recognize this place. Remembering that the pictures in Grandma's bedroom looked better if he wasn't too close to them, he pushed himself away from the table. Wincing in pain, he steadied himself against the sideboard and took another look at the painting. Think, he ordered himself. Think.

What he saw filled him with dread. He was almost certain that he was looking at a view of the river he and his parents had driven beside on Sunday. It was after they'd signed up for the white-water rafting. Dad had suggested that they take a drive along the winding road that followed the river's path, to get an idea of where they'd be going in three days' time.

They'd stopped several times to watch other rafters bobbing along in the churning, racing water. At one spot, Pete had noticed a small cabin flanked by four tall tamaracks.

That scene re-formed in his mind like a developing photo. First, he recalled the cabin and the pines, then the cluster of white birches, the cedar shingles, the three large boulders at the river's edge, and the sharp bend just before the rapids. His memory offered up a snapshot that perfectly matched the painting.

His heart skipped a beat. Vague new fears tugged at the corners of his mind, pushing him to think the unthinkable — that the picture was waiting to reveal a terrible secret. A secret that was hidden in the only bare patch of canvas left to be filled in.

Pete sat back down at the table. His fingers felt weak and clumsy as he struggled to pry the lids off the last two unused containers — a fiery orange and a bright royal blue.

With a trembling hand, he stirred each colour. Then he forced himself to dip the brush and apply orange to the four small shapes labelled 19. He wiped off the brush and held it over the blue pot. Then, one last time, he dipped the tip into the paint, and slowly filled in the two strips of blue dividing the small sections of orange.

With the last bit of blue in place, the secret was no more. Part of what Pete had thought was a log jutting out into the rapids could now be seen for what it was — the upper part of a body slumped over the log. The orange and blue life jacket outlined its shape clearly, as did the shadow of a leg trailing just under the surface of the water.

As a sickening certainty washed over Pete, Mr. Kramer pushed open the screen door. When Pete saw the look on his face, he knew that he was right — something terrible had happened.

"What's wrong? Tell me, please!" Pete shouted frantically. For a moment, the lodge owner looked confused as well as troubled.

"Tell me," Pete insisted, pushing himself up from the table. "Where are Mom and Dad?"

"Take it easy, son, or you'll open up those stitches," Mr. Kramer began, moving quickly to Pete's side. "Here, lean on me. Let's go sit down for a sec."

"I don't want to sit down," Pete said, his voice breaking. "I just want to know where Mom and Dad are."

"Your mom's safe, Pete. The park warden just called. She'll be fine, so don't you worry about her."

"And my dad?"

Mr. Kramer spoke gently, "There's been an accident, son. Seems the raft capsized shooting the second set of rapids. Everything would have been fine if the guide hadn't hit his head. But with him knocked out, people had to fend for themselves. They did well, though. Managed to get the guide to shore. But . . ."

Mr. Kramer paused to collect himself. He swallowed and took a deep breath, then went on, ". . . but they couldn't find your dad, son. He's . . . missing. Must have been swept down the river." Pete began to shake.

"Listen to me, son. They're bringing in the helicopters right now. They should be here soon, and there's still at least two hours of light left. The other rafters are already searching. So, don't go thinking the worst just yet because . . ."

"But," Pete interrupted, "I know where he is!"

"Now, now, son. Listen to me . . ."

"No, you've got to listen to me. I know where he is. See?" Pete held up the painting and pointed to the life jacket. "Look, just look."

Mr. Kramer leaned forward and peered at the picture.

"No," Pete ordered, "don't come too close. Here," he said, taking two steps back. "Now, look again."

Mr. Kramer stared. Suddenly, his eyes widened. "Why, that's the old Olliver place, down by Trout Bend. Where'd you get this?"

Pete was frantic. How could he possibly explain what had happened? It would take too long.

"That doesn't matter right now. Please, Mr. Kramer. I just know that's where Dad is. We've got to get to him."

"Well," Mr. Kramer began, "I'm not sure that this makes any sense, but . . . okay, it can't hurt to take a drive out to Trout Bend, if that'll make you feel better."

Pete stumbled toward the door. "Hurry, Mr. Kramer, hurry," he pleaded, pulling the lodge owner after him.

Fifteen minutes later, Mr. Kramer was dragging Pete's dad up the bank to where Pete sat, holding his leg. Pete had slipped scrambling down the hill toward the fiery orange life jacket they'd spotted from the truck, and his leg was bleeding again. But he was feeling no pain.

Since the moment Mr. Kramer shouted, "Your dad's breathing, son. He's breathing!" Pete had felt only incredible relief. That, and the urge to shout to the treetops, "I heard you, too, Grandpa. I heard you."

THE RAVEN

Cito would never admit it to most of his friends, but he actually liked hanging out at the library. It was better than being stuck at home with a babysitter while his mom went to night school.

For him, the library held happy memories of Saturday morning story hours and puppet shows when he was little. And he always felt a thrill of anticipation when new arrivals showed up on the paperback racks.

One night, he found a Gordon Korman and another evening he discovered Daniel Pinkwater, who also came up with the kind of stories he loved to read. He even managed to catch up on his homework.

He liked the building, too. With its high ceilings, dark wood panelling and cushioned window seats, it reminded him of a castle or a mansion in a movie.

Then the bird arrived — and ruined everything.

It was the first thing Cito noticed when he walked in that night. It sat perched on a tall pedestal to one side of the arched entrance to the children's section.

What's this? he wondered when he spotted it. A new security guard waiting to swoop down on book snatchers? When he got closer, though, he realized that the bird's swooping days had ended long ago.

It was big. And it looked even bigger mounted on the branch that served as a stand. Its ruffled black feathers had lost their sheen and its dull slate-grey toes ending in long, curved claws looked dry and brittle. One of the stiff wing feathers was bent near the tip and poked out at an awkward angle. But the fine feathers covering the head were sleek and smooth and the slightly parted beak seemed poised to emit a screeching cry.

It was the beady yellow eyes, though, that bothered Cito the most. They seemed to glow with an eerie light all their own. He stared up at them as he sidled past and they stared back, cold and menacing.

Creepy, he thought, as he slipped into a chair and dropped his writing folder onto the table in front of him. He needed to come up with a third verse for a poem that was due the next day.

How about, "Crow, crow, go away. Stand in front of a Chevrolet?" he mused, stealing another peek at the sinister sentinel. He felt as if its eyes were following his every move.

Why don't you go read a book or something? he asked silently, and turned back to his work.

He sensed Miss O'Toole, the librarian, standing behind him even before she spoke.

"So, it's poetry tonight, is it?" she asked. Then she smiled and pointed at the bird, "I'm sure you'll write a great poem with him here."

Cito frowned. What on earth was she talking about?

"He helped a writer before, you know," Miss O'Toole

added, "or at least we think he did. The research isn't complete yet, so we're not absolutely sure, but it looks as though this is the same stuffed bird that once shared a room with Edgar Allan Poe. Mr. Herzig — he runs the antique store around the corner on Peckford — discovered it. When he suggested displaying it here, we were delighted."

Seeing the puzzled look on Cito's face, she paused. "You've heard of Poe?"

Cito suddenly recognized the name. "Oh yeah," he said. "Poe. He made horror movies, right? Like the one about the guy who accidentally buries his sister alive in a tomb in the house and she finally claws her way out. Then, when the guy sees her standing there all bloody and everything, he goes crazy and they both fall down dead and their mansion crashes down on top of them. He did that one, didn't he?"

Miss O'Toole was smiling. "That sounds a bit like 'The Fall of the House of Usher.'"

"Yeah, that's the one. The special effects are pretty good for an old movie. I've seen it twice . . . it's sort of scary, isn't it?"

"I'm sure it is. I haven't seen the movie. But I have read the story and I remember it very well. Edgar Allan Poe wrote it more than a hundred and fifty years ago."

"Uh oh." Cito felt foolish. "Then he couldn't have made the movie, huh?"

"No, but he did write some pretty scary stories that have been made into movies. I'm pretty sure there's a film version of 'The Pit and the Pendulum,' too."

"Oh yeah, that was gross," Cito blurted out excitedly.

"It had all those rats and that axe swinging over the guy's head and the walls squishing in around him."

"So you do know Poe."

"Well, I've never read his books or anything."

"And you probably wouldn't like them too much just yet. The writing is very old-fashioned and they have lots of description, and you're more of an action story fan, aren't you?"

Cito nodded.

"But Poe wrote poetry as well," she added.

"That's funny," Cito chuckled.

Miss O'Toole caught on instantly and laughed, too. "You're right, but most of his poems weren't funny — especially not the one about him." She pointed at the bird again.

No wonder, Cito thought as he looked up at the huge crow. There's nothing funny about him. He's horrible.

With its wings folded against its body and its head cocked to one side, the bird seemed to be listening to the conversation. For a moment, Cito was transfixed. He felt trapped in the evil glare glowing from the creature's cold, yellow eyes.

Miss O'Toole's voice broke the spell.

"The poem is about a man who's very sad and lonely because the love of his life, Lenore, has died. One night, he's all alone in his room. He hears knocks at the door and tapping sounds at the window, but nobody's there.

"Finally, he opens the window and a big black bird walks in and perches over his doorway. At first, the man's happy for the company. But then the bird starts to drive

him crazy because it keeps saying the same word over and over."

Cito shuddered. He didn't want to hear any more. But Miss O'Toole kept talking.

"Mr. Herzig says that all the evidence he's collected so far shows that this is the same stuffed bird that was in the furnished room Poe was renting when he wrote the poem about Lenore. Looking at it all the time inspired him to write it. Isn't that exciting?"

Luckily, Cito didn't need to answer. At that moment, Mr. Leno came over from the reference desk to ask Miss O'Toole for help.

That night, the bird's menacing presence distracted Cito so much that he changed seats three times. No matter where he moved, it seemed to be watching him.

At one point, he deliberately sat with his back to it, but that just made things worse. Even when he couldn't see them, he felt the spying, prying yellow eyes boring into the back of his neck. No matter what he did, he couldn't shake off the eerie feeling that there was something unnatural about the bird, something that made his hair stand on end.

When Cito arrived at the library the next Tuesday, he headed straight for the cushions across from the aquarium. As he passed the bird, he kept his head turned away so he didn't have to look at it. He leaned back into the cushions and relaxed, watching the angelfish playing follow-the-leader though the elodea.

"Can't get me here," he whispered triumphantly. He opened his book and started reading.

But he had spoken too soon. When he looked up, a black reflection was shimmering on the glass of the aquarium. The beady eyes and parted beak were unmistakable.

Impossible, Cito thought. It's too far away, and the angle is all wrong. He closed his eyes, then looked again. The image of the bird was still there.

He scrambled off the cushions and made for the empty window seat on the other side of the room. Miss O'Toole raised a warning eyebrow when he banged into a chair on the way.

"Oops," he whispered. Out of the corner of his eye, he stole a quick glance at the bird and was relieved to see that its head was turned in the opposite direction. But his relief was short-lived.

Like someone who keeps bending a sprained finger hoping to find that it has stopped hurting, Cito kept checking on the raven. The next time he looked, he realized that he could see part of its right eye. Moments later, the whole eye was visible. When he looked again, he could see both eyes. Slowly but surely, the bird had turned its head. Its stare carried an unspoken threat that made his blood run cold.

He turned away quickly and blinked several times. When he looked back, the bird's wing tips were quivering and rising ever so slightly. It's trying to fly, he told himself. But it can't. It's dead.

The piercing shriek that followed was more than Cito could handle. He clapped his hands over his ears and crouched on the window seat, waiting to feel the talons he was sure were about to sink into his neck.

Instead, he felt a hand tugging at his arm and heard Miss O'Toole saying, "Don't be afraid. It's just the fire alarm. Stay calm and walk over to the door with me. Come on now. Let's go."

Cito struggled to his feet, feeling ridiculous. Then he smelled the smoke. He snatched up his backpack and followed the librarian and the other kids she was herding toward the front door. As he passed under the archway, he couldn't resist taking a last peek at the bird. What he saw stopped him in his tracks.

It was no longer staring at him. Its eyes were shifting from side to side, its wings were quivering, and its beak was opening and closing, as if it were trying to speak.

"Miss O'Toole, look," Cito croaked, pointing at the raven.

"What? Is someone else back there? Where?"

"There," Cito pointed.

"Oh, Cito, this is no time to worry about the bird. Come on, let's go."

As Miss O'Toole nudged him toward the exit, he heard it — a low squawking sound. Again and again, all the way to the door, it echoed faintly above the din. It was the bird's voice, of that he was certain, and it kept squawking what sounded like one word — "Nevermore."

A month later, the library reopened. The fire had been a small one, confined to the area between the main desk and the arch. And although Cito was wary of returning, he'd had his fill of Mrs. Fonseca, the babysitter Mom had found. So, two days after the library opened its doors again, Cito was back.

When he walked in, the first thing he noticed was the new carpeting. The old oak counter that had served as the front desk was gone, too. It had been replaced by a sleek white one that angled off on each side to form a U-shape.

And over near the archway on the right, where the

pedestal had stood, was a large new revolving stand bulging with paperbacks. Cito scanned the rest of the main floor. The bird was nowhere to be seen.

He breathed a sigh of relief and headed for the big table. He sat down and dug out his history notebook, ready to study for a test he had the next day.

But try as he might, he couldn't concentrate. He found himself looking up every now and then, as if to make sure the bird was really gone. Good riddance, he thought.

But he couldn't get it out of his mind. He could still see the piercing eyes, the shuddering wings, the gaping beak — and he could still hear the horrible squawk.

Miss O'Toole slipped into the chair beside him.

"The bird was lost in the fire," she said, as if reading his mind. "I felt terrible leaving it behind . . . and I felt even worse explaining what happened to Mr. Herzig. Luckily, he wasn't nearly as upset as I thought he would be."

"How come?" Cito asked.

"Well, it seems that the bird wasn't Poe's raven after all. Mr. Herzig was terribly disappointed. When all the evidence was added up, he realized he was wrong. Apparently, our bird was just somebody's worthless old stuffed crow."

Cito frowned. He wasn't so sure. "What if Mr. Herzig was right?" he began cautiously. "What if the evidence was wrong?"

Miss O'Toole smiled indulgently. "No, Cito. I'm afraid that's just wishful thinking."

As she stood up to leave, Cito suddenly knew what he had to do. He stopped her with a question.

"Wait. Can you show me where to find that poem you told me about?"

"Of course. Come with me."

Cito followed her as she wound through the aisles in the main stacks.

"It should be in here," she said, pulling a fat book off the shelf. "Yes, here it is, 'The Raven.'"

Cito took the book back to his table, spread it open and began to read.

The first line wasn't too bad. "Once upon a midnight dreary, while I pondered, weak and weary" was easy enough to follow and it had a nice ring to it, too. But it was downhill after that.

Cito got the part about someone tapping at the chamber door and the bit about Lenore, but he had trouble making sense of the other long, rambling lines.

Frustrated, he turned the page. The raven finally showed up in the seventh verse.

He struggled on. "Ghastly and grim," it said. Poe had that right, he thought.

Then his heart skipped a beat. The word leaped out from the end of the next verse. He stared to make sure he was really seeing it.

Cito ran a shaky finger down the next two pages. There it was, at the end of every one of the next ten verses. The word the raven kept repeating — "Nevermore."

Cito stared as the words blurred and a vision swam before his eyes. His head was spinning. He saw a man sitting at a desk in a cold, dark room. The only light came from the flickering embers of a dying fire. The man was scribbling furiously, his eyes blazing with fear. A huge black bird was mounted on a stand behind him. It was screeching one word — "Nevermore."

"Cito?"

Cito jumped.

"Sorry," said Miss O'Toole. "I didn't mean to startle you. I was just wondering if you found what you were looking for."

"Uh, yes, thanks," Cito mumbled, handing her the book. "I don't need this anymore."

Anymore. Nevermore. Poor Lenore. The words bounced around his head. Poor Poe, he thought, stuck in a room with that . . . thing!

And poor Mr. Herzig, he thought. But it's just as well he doesn't know that he had Poe's bird all along. He'd be so disappointed that it's gone. But I'm not, he thought, as he stood up to leave. I never want to see that bird again. Nevermore.

BOTTOM OF THE NINTH

Donny Adams wasn't just a fan. He was a believer. He didn't just cheer on his team, hoping they'd win. He believed they'd win — but only if he did his part, too.

It hadn't always been that way. When he was nine, Donny had been content to be a spectator. It had been fun to put on his new Condors cap and take in a few games with Dad. They would munch their way through a big bag of peanuts, stand up every time the wave rolled by, cheer wildly whenever a Condor got a hit, and sing along with the crowd whenever the loudspeakers blared "Take Me Out to the Ball Game."

The next year was even better. For Donny's tenth birthday, Dad surprised him with tickets to five home games — the best seats in the stadium, behind home plate.

The Condors won all five games, doubling Donny's excitement and pleasure. He sat spellbound through each one, watching the players' every move and learning everything he could about them and the game itself. He wore his cap to each game and waved the copper-and-gold Condors pennant he'd bought with his own money.

Donny kept the pennant in a place of honour over his bed, beside the team picture he'd carefully cut out of the newspaper. And, whenever he could find the time, he watched his favourite team play on TV.

The Condors did well that year, finishing second in their division. But what was good for the Condors was bad for Donny. The next year, more fans bought season's tickets, making it harder to get good seats in advance. Ticket prices went up, too. That spring, Donny and Dad managed to take in four games, but they sat in the bleachers high above left field. When the Condors lost every one of these games, Donny told Dad he'd just as soon not go to Baylor Field anymore.

"It's not much fun sitting up in the nosebleeds," he'd explained. "You can't really see the game."

This was true, as far as it went. But Donny had another reason for not wanting to go, one he didn't share with Dad. The way he saw it, when he was sitting behind home plate, the Condors had won. When he sat in the bleachers, they lost. The least he could do was to stop bringing his team bad luck. He'd stay home for the rest of the season and cheer them on in front of the TV. If that helps them win, it'll be worth it, he decided.

But there were some days early that summer when Donny wondered if the price of a Condors' victory wasn't a little high. Gone was the fun of sitting with Dad among thousands of other fans, eating peanuts, smelling popcorn, doing the wave. Gone, too, were the many afternoons he might have spent tossing a ball, going to a movie or just goofing off with his friends. Whenever he had to choose between his friends and a ball game, he chose the game. After a while, his friends just stopped calling him.

Once, he tried inviting some of them over to his house to watch a game with him. This had been his mother's idea. But Raoul had cheered for the Gators, Jason kept grabbing the remote and changing the channel to see how the wrestling was going, and Brad had teased him about arranging his pennant and the cards of the players in the Condors' starting lineup on the coffee table. The Gators won that afternoon, and Donny was pretty sure he knew why.

"They ruined everything," he complained to his mother later.

"Is that how you see it?" Mom had asked. "Maybe you should take a closer look at yourself," she added tersely, before leaving him alone to tidy up the living room.

What's with her? he wondered as he straightened the cushions and collected the empty pop cans. I didn't do anything. They just don't understand, and neither does she. Neither, he realized a week later, did his dad or his younger brother, Ian.

The next Thursday evening was picture-perfect, as only a late July evening could be. Mom was on the back porch stripping paint off an old kitchen chair, and Dad and Ian were off on a bike ride. Donny had turned down their invitation to go along. He had to get ready for the game.

"Come on. It'll be fun. We'll be back before dark," Dad had said. "The game can wait just this once, can't it?"

"Not for Donny, it can't," Ian piped up. "He's baseball crazy."

"Am not."

"Are so."

"Wrong. I just don't want to go anywhere with a snot-nosed little . . ."

"Stop it, you two," Mr. Adams interrupted, and hustled Ian out the door.

Good riddance, Donny thought, as he went upstairs to collect his good luck charms. He came back down wearing his Condors cap and carrying his pennant, a pile of trading cards and a poster of high-octane starter Billy Batista. The poster was a last-minute addition, but Batista had pitched a shutout the last time he'd gotten the call, so Donny felt sure having his poster out would bring him luck on the mound.

It was the bottom of the third inning when Dad and Ian returned to find Donny waving his pennant and shouting, "Yes. Yes. Yes!"

"So, I take it we're doing okay," Dad said, pushing aside Batista's poster so he could sit down on the couch beside Donny.

"Don't move . . . uh, I mean, could you please leave this here, Dad?" Donny asked nervously, propping the picture back against the cushion beside him.

Suddenly, he shouted, "Don't you dare, you little creep!"

Ian had been reaching toward one of the cards on the coffee table. He pulled back his hand as if stung.

"Sor-reee," Ian drawled. "I just wanted to read about Klein's numbers, that's all."

"They're not numbers, idiot," Donny lashed back. "They're stats. And you wouldn't understand them anyway. You don't know anything."

"That's enough, Donny," Dad interrupted icily.

"But, Dad, Klein wasn't up to bat yet," Donny rattled on defensively. "You can't touch his card when he's not up to bat. There, see what Ian did," he added, pointing to the television. "See? Klein just struck out. He brought him bad luck, right?"

"Ian didn't do that, Donny. But you did plenty. It's apology time, mister."

Feeling trapped, Donny mumbled grudgingly, "I'm sorry."

Dad sighed, "Now, fellas, what do you say we all sit down and enjoy the rest of this game?"

"Sounds good to me," Ian bounced over and snuggled up beside his father. Mr. Adams patted the space on his other side and said, "There's plenty of room here for you, too, Donny."

But Donny didn't see it that way. It won't be any fun watching the game with you, he thought. You just don't understand. Nobody does.

Aloud, he said curtly, "Thanks, but no thanks." Then he picked up his cards, grabbed his poster and headed for the basement.

His mother opened the back door just as he reached the top of the stairs.

"Wait, Donny. What was all that shouting about?" she asked.

"Nothing," Donny grunted.

"Well, it was a pretty noisy nothing. And where are you going with all that stuff?"

"Downstairs, to watch the game on Grandpa's old TV. Or isn't that allowed?"

"Oh, it's allowed, but it doesn't sound like much fun. Where's your dad, and Ian?"

"In there," Donny said angrily, pointing to the living room. "They wrecked everything."

"Now where have I heard that before? Let me think," Mrs. Adams said. "Could it be someone named Donny who said it when . . . ?"

She got no further.

"Can I go now?" Donny interrupted.

"Sure, but tell me, have I missed something here? I thought baseball was supposed to be fun. You don't seem to be having too much fun these days, Donny."

"Well, I will if I can get back to the game," he snapped, and started down the stairs.

Most of the basement was just that — a basement. But one corner had been set aside as a play area. There was a square of carpet on the floor, an old recliner and two lawn chairs to sit on, shelves for toys, a coffee table much the worse for wear, and the TV set Grandpa had left behind when he gave up his apartment and drove off to Florida in a new motorhome.

Donny switched on the TV and tuned in the game. He propped the Batista poster in front of the coffee table and flopped into the recliner. Leaning forward, he arranged his cards according to the starting lineup. He jammed his pennant into the space beside the chair's pop-up footrest, and settled back to watch. The way I want to, he thought. The way I have to, a faint voice whispered at the back of his mind. He quickly tuned this out and concentrated on the game.

With no one around to bother him, he was free to wave, cheer, hold up cards, cover his eyes, even stand on his head if that's what it took. This is great, he thought.

And, when the Condors came from behind to win in the ninth, he decided not to watch baseball upstairs again.

Before the next game, Donny headed for the basement to prepare. Remembering the winning formula he'd used on Thursday, he turned on the TV, propped up his posters — Calvin Green's as well as Batista's — positioned the chair, sat down, arranged the starting lineup, and jammed the pennant into place.

We're ready, he told himself. This is going to be fun. He checked his watch. Five minutes to go. It occurred to him that this was just enough time to make some popcorn.

Leaving his cap behind on the chair, he whipped upstairs, put a bag of popcorn into the microwave, set the timer and waited impatiently for the buzzer to sound.

Then he raced back downstairs, put his cap back on and settled into the recliner. "Let's play ball," he announced as the players took to the field. The Condors won handily.

Then, just when it looked as if the team and Donny were doing everything right and the Condors might actually take their division, things started going terribly wrong.

The team set out on a twelve-game road trip and lost five in a row. Desperately, Donny tinkered with his rules for bringing off a Condors' win until he could barely keep track of them. He became a boy possessed as the preparations before each game escalated into a frantic race to get everything done in time.

He was also worried that something he'd done had caused the string of defeats. Was the popcorn all gone when Batista loaded the bases and threw the lollipop that Feliciano had drilled high over the right-field wall? Should he eat it more slowly the next time, or should he forget it altogether? Maybe that would do the trick.

As the next game approached, Donny realized he was in trouble. His eyes blurred as he turned on the TV, and his hands trembled as he tried to organize the Condors' cards into their starting lineup. I can't take it anymore, he suddenly found himself thinking. He threw down the cards, slumped into the recliner and closed his eyes.

His head was spinning.

This is too much. I don't care, he thought. No, I do care. The Condors have to win. They just have to. But Ian was right . . . and so were Mom and Dad. This is crazy, he thought. It isn't fun anymore. It's become a nightmare, a nightmare that has to stop.

Donny opened his eyes. But the real nightmare had just begun.

On the coffee table, the starting lineup was neatly arranged. His posters were propped up on both sides of the TV. The pennants were in place, too, and his T-shirt was draped over the arm of the chair, with his cap balanced carefully on top of it. Everything was set up, ready for the game to start — but he hadn't done any of it.

His heart began to pound. He reached for his cap, ready to heave it across the room. But he couldn't. Instead, he felt his hand moving toward his head. Like a zombie following its master's orders, he put on his cap, flinching at its touch. This favourite of all his treasures had become a thing of horror, something that made his skin crawl.

Terrified, Donny tried to fling himself out of the chair. I have to get out of here, he thought. But he couldn't move. An invisible force threatened to crush him each time he tried to push himself up.

Desperate, he opened his mouth to scream for help, but no sound emerged. Finally, he stopped struggling and collapsed limply in the chair. The game started. Through no choice of his own, he began to watch.

His last clear thought was that he hadn't made the popcorn. After that, everything blurred. He could see the TV and hear the announcers' voices, but the picture and the words were hideously distorted.

Donny was terrified. He felt trapped in a kind of waking-dead zone where nothing made any sense . . . until two familiar words finally pierced the horrible blur.

Donny latched onto them like a drowning swimmer clutching a life preserver. He forced himself to focus on the familiar syllables. "Cracker Jacks." Then, an entire line echoed in his head — "I don't care if I never come back . . . don't care if I never come back . . . don't care . . . care . . . care."

But I do care, he screamed silently. I want to come back. Suddenly, Donny realized that he could hear again — and see. On the TV screen, the crowd was on its feet, roaring out the words to "Take Me Out to the Ball Game."

Donny felt weak with relief. Without thinking, he reached up to scratch his head. As his hand touched the brim of his cap, the full impact of what he'd just done hit him. He'd moved on his own. Slowly, he lowered his arm and leaned forward. Then he carefully pushed himself out of the chair.

To reassure himself that the nightmare had truly ended, he ran a quick reality check. He focused on the screen, where a chart listed the runs, hits and errors for the first eight innings. He was able to read it and understand what it meant.

It showed that the Condors were behind by two runs. Too bad, he thought. He tensed, waiting for the frantic feeling that he had to do something to make his team win, but it didn't come.

He steadied himself against the coffee table and stepped away from the chair. Still nervous, he glanced back at the television. Farley, the Condors' star reliever, was winding up. The ball burned across the outside corner of the plate and Carter, the Falcons' slugger, was history.

Donny found himself hoping that the Condors would pull the game out of the fire when they got up to bat. Then he caught himself. It was bad luck to think of winning, wasn't it? No, it was bad luck only if you said your team was going to win when they were leading, not when they were behind. Besides, you had to say it out loud to jinx them. That's what Dad said, anyway. He said all baseball fans knew better than to jinx their team that way.

With this thought, Donny began to smile. One or two superstitions were okay. That was part of the fun of baseball.

He switched off the TV, picked up his pennant and headed upstairs, hoping he'd find Dad or Ian watching the game in the living room. He still wanted to see the bottom of the ninth, but it would be more fun if he could watch it with somebody.

THE EMPTY PLACE

Mom pointed to the large hawk soaring above the cottage. "Look, Kit. Isn't it beautiful?" Kit glanced skyward.

"So what?" she said sullenly. "It's just a bird." She turned her back and began to walk away.

"Kit? Where are you going?"

"Nowhere." Kit kept walking.

"Hold on, Kit. It's nearly lunchtime. I want you to stay close to the cottage for now."

Kit took two more steps, then stopped as her little brother, Eugene, dashed out of the bushes beside the cottage. He came straight at her, arms outstretched.

"Hey, Kit, look what I found."

Carefully, he uncupped his hands. But not carefully enough. A bumpy brown toad leapt out just as Kit bent down to look.

"You brat," she hissed, jumping back.

"But, Kit, I never did it on purpose. Come on. Help me catch it again, will you?"

"You wish. Catch your own stupid toads — and keep them far away from me." Kit turned on her heel and stomped away.

"You're no fun anymore," Eugene yelled as he headed

back behind the cottage, hot on the trail of the escaping amphibian.

His words pierced Kit with a guilt that nearly stopped her in her tracks. She knew she was acting like a jerk, but this knowledge just made her angrier — with herself and everybody else.

Tears stung her eyes. She hadn't asked to be included in the family's vacation at the cottage. In fact, she'd begged to stay behind in town, where she could watch TV, hang out with her friends and have some fun.

Kit kept walking. She wanted a space of her own, away from the rest of the family. She started to jog, then broke into a run.

"Kit, wait," she heard her mother call. Kit ignored her and kept running until she reached the cover of a nearby willow grove.

From her vantage point under the drooping branches, Kit watched her parents walk back to the picnic table and sit down. Eugene was already seated, getting a head start on the sandwiches.

"Guess who's missing from the happy holiday picture?" Kit muttered angrily. They're just fine, she thought. They can have lots of fun without me.

Turning away, she began to work her way through the willow branches. When she broke through to the other side of the grove, she took a deep breath and took off across the vast expanse of meadow that lay before her.

Kit ran and ran. She ran until her breathing was so harsh and shallow that she could run no more. She slowed to a jog, but finally had to stop. Gasping, she bent over, hands on her knees, and tried to catch her breath.

Gradually, the pounding in her chest lessened, and the pain in her side eased. She straightened up slowly and looked back the way she'd come. Far off, to the right, she could still see the dark outline of the woods ringing the lake, but she could barely pick out the cottage and the willow grove beside it.

Not far enough. I can still see it, Kit thought, and decided to keep going. "Until I don't have to see anyone or anything," she said aloud as she set off once more, this time at an easy jog.

She had no idea how long she'd been running when she started to pay attention to her surroundings again. The first thing she noticed was that the sun was no longer directly overhead. She could still feel its powerful rays on the back of her neck and shoulders, but it was definitely lower in the sky. Her lengthening shadow told her that.

Glancing down, she realized that the ground had changed, too. The soft meadow grasses were gone and, underfoot, dried weeds and withering wild strawberry plants crunched and crackled.

The sun's cooking you too, she mused, looking at the brown and red leaves clinging to a sandy patch of ground before her. Suddenly, a quick shadow streaked across her path. Kit turned and squinted over her shoulder into the sky.

Oh, it's you, she thought as she picked the large black hawk out of the sun's glare. Who invited you along? Go back to my mother. She's the bird lover, not me. Aloud she added, "This is my spot. Mine, you hear."

The realization that she had actually shouted these

words left Kit feeling more than a little foolish.

Thank goodness no one is around to hear, she thought. But the words had struck a memory chord. Kit stopped walking and looked around again.

Hey, maybe this really is my place, she thought, recalling the game she'd invented when she was little. She flopped onto the ground, thinking that she might finally be able to win it here.

Kit stretched out and began to move her eyes in every direction while keeping her head perfectly still.

"Nearly," she said, sitting up and yanking at a tall clump of chicory that had managed to survive the heat and sand. "Sorry, but you have to go," she announced. Then she lay back down and looked around again.

That's better, she thought. This place has definite possibilities. Then she saw the hawk again.

"Go away," she ordered. "This is my place. You're wrecking the game."

The hawk lingered briefly, suddenly swooped lower, then soared high and faded into the cloudless sky.

Finally, Kit thought. Nobody and nothing. I've finally found my empty place.

Her thoughts drifted back to the summer six years ago when she'd started her search for this place. That year, her family had spent their vacation at her uncle's farm. One day, lying on the roof of the cowshed with her cousins, Kit had found herself staring into an empty, clear blue sky. She had lain outside many times before — flat on her back on the apartment balcony, in the wading pool at the park, and even in the schoolyard. But this time was different.

This time, nothing, absolutely nothing had broken her view of the sky — no birds, no branches, no awnings, not even a hydro pole or telephone line. Suddenly, she'd been overwhelmed by the vast emptiness.

This is fun, she'd thought. It's like being all alone in the middle of nowhere, even though I'm really not. It felt good, being in the empty place she'd just discovered.

Keeping her head still, she'd let her eyes wander to the left. Still nothing. Once again, all she could see was blue. When she'd looked to the right, though, a tall tree had intruded into the blueness. Then two crows had risen squawking from the garden, flying directly into view, and the spell had been broken.

But the excitement of that moment had lingered. Several times that summer, she'd searched for a place where she could lie down, look up and around and see nothing but sky. It became a kind of game for her. She'd flop down, cushion her head with her hands, and try out a new place. But, no matter where she tried out the view, something — a tree or a bird or a single power line — always got in the way.

There was no point even trying on cloudy days. She would not allow the smallest wisp of white to drift by. That was against the rules, rules she'd come up with after that time on the cowshed roof. Only the sun was allowed. She couldn't look right at it anyway, so it didn't count. But anything else would break the spell cast by the emptiness.

When her cousins began to tease her about lying around all the time, just staring at the sky, she quickly learned to seek out her empty place only when she was alone. She came close sometimes, but she never did find it that summer.

When she returned to the city, thoughts of her summer quest faded. Once, in the winter, she had tried again at the park, after an unusually heavy snowfall. The sun was shining brightly and the park was blanketed in white. She lay down in the snow and looked all around but, try as she might, she could never eliminate the nearby high-rises from the picture. No matter where she went in the park, she could still see at least one.

The next summer Kit gave up her search. She was lying with two of her friends on the teeter-totters in the park. The three of them were just lying there saying nothing, staring up at the sky.

When she asked them if they ever tried to find a place where they could see absolutely nothing but the sky, they looked at her as if she had grown antennae. "You're nuts, Kit," one of them had said. Embarrassed, Kit had vowed never to think about the stupid game again.

But here she was, two years later, absolutely spellbound because there was nothing, absolutely nothing, in sight. This is amazing, she thought. Nothing and nobody. Just what I wanted. I wonder how long it will last.

Now that she knew it was possible to find such a place, a new rule began to take shape in her mind. Once I find it, I can't move until something invades it, she thought.

"But that won't take long," she added aloud. "Something always comes along."

Kit lay still, staring upward at the seamless blue canopy, waiting for that something — a plane, a cloud, a bee buzzing by. She waited and waited, but nothing intruded into her empty place.

"Amazing," she repeated softly, relishing the moment.

Then her neck began to itch. Bet I've got a sunburn, she found herself thinking. Hope Mom brought the Noxzema. Don't be silly. Mom always remembers to bring the Noxzema . . . and the sun block.

Mom always remembers the air mattress, too. And a brand new jigsaw puzzle. Always a new puzzle. Wonder how many pieces this one will have? And the new game?

What'll it be? Balderdash? We don't have that yet. Gotta wait to find out, though. It has to be a surprise . . .

Kit realized she was looking forward to finding out which games Mom had brought along. Okay, so maybe doing puzzles and playing games with the family isn't so bad, she thought. Maybe I won't be totally bored out of my mind.

Kit scanned the empty sky again. Her neck was getting stiff, and she wanted to stand up and brush away the sand that was starting to make her skin itch. Okay, I've had enough. Time for something to break into the emptiness. Time to go home.

"Come out, come out, wherever you are," she called.

Maybe I goofed. Maybe I can see something, she thought, and forced her eyes from side to side as far as they could go. But she'd picked her spot well. Without turning her head, she couldn't see past the sandy patch where she had flopped down.

How long have I been here? she wondered. A long time. Shouldn't have pulled out that plant. Then I could have seen it — and I could have got up. Maybe I'll cheat. Turn my head a bit. I'm sure there was some tall grass just past the strawberry leaves. I remember that.

She checked the sky one last time. Empty. That's it, then. Time's up, she decided, and turned her head to the side. No tall grass there. She turned the other way. There was nothing there either.

"That's weird," Kit said softly. I was sure it was there, she thought. Oh well, I moved my head so the game's over anyway. I may as well get up.

Kit sat up and looked around. She rubbed her eyes and looked again.

Impossible, she thought, and scrambled to her feet.

She stared in disbelief. For as far as she could see, there was absolutely nothing, nothing but the occasional wild strawberry runner clinging to the dry brown ground. It was as if this empty spot had spread out around her until it met the sky. The sweat trickling down her neck felt suddenly cold. It sent a shiver up her spine.

For a long time, Kit stood transfixed. Then she began to turn slowly, desperately scanning the horizon for anything that would help her get her bearings. She became frantic, looking — and looking again — for a familiar landmark. All she could see were acres of sand meeting the endless blue of the empty sky.

Feeling dizzy, she stopped turning and looked up again. The sun still shone, but it was much lower in the sky. Still, it couldn't help her. She had no idea whether the cottage lay north, south, east or west.

She wanted to run again. But she didn't know which way to go. For the second time that day, Kit felt like crying. She broke into sobs, feeling very lost and alone.

She had no idea how much time had passed when she began to notice the breeze brushing against her tears. Gentle at first, it grew stronger with each gust. Thick white clouds edged with grey began to roll in, gobbling up the blue. Kit's heart raced. She could smell the approaching storm. Run, her mind screamed. Run. Run. Run.

Kit started to run, then turned and began to run in the opposite direction. "Which way? Which way?" she yelled into the terrible emptiness. Despairing, she stopped again, choking back her sobs.

It was then that she saw it. It was only a speck at first, a pinpoint of black in one of the last remaining patches of blue. When it disappeared behind a cloud, Kit thought she'd imagined it. But, seconds later, it was back, soaring and diving, its widespread wings riding the wind. Closer and closer it came, until it was directly overhead. It hovered for a moment, suspended in space. Then, with a mighty flap of its wings, it veered sharply back into the wind, struggling to return the way it had come.

Suddenly Kit realized where it had come from — and she knew where it was going. The voice inside her head became a chorus. Run. Run. Run. Kit began to run again, this time after the hawk.

They were going home.

PASSWORD TO MYSTERY

I like my little sister, Jasmine. She's okay for a seven-year-old. So when I saw how upset she was that Mom didn't believe her, I felt I had to do something. For her sake — and for Mom's, too — I had to find out what really happened the day the garage burned down.

It wasn't that Mom — or anybody else — blamed Jasmine for the fire. The fire inspector said afterwards that a possum probably ate through the wiring and the old wooden building just went up like a tinderbox.

Besides, Jasmine wasn't anywhere near the garage when the fire started. And that's really what caused all the trouble — and plunked us into the middle of a mystery straight out of *The Twilight Zone*.

After school, Mrs. Bellamy, our next-door neighbour, babysits Jasmine until Mom gets home. When Karen and David Bellamy, who go to a different school, get home, the three of them — Jasmine, Karen and David — go out and play.

Most days they play . . . well, used to play . . . in our garage. We don't have a car anymore, so Mom let us kids use it. There was a bench, three chairs, a table, an old radio and a bunch of other stuff in there.

On the day of the fire, the garage was already toast — burnt toast — by the time Mom got home from work. Fire trucks were everywhere.

The first thing Mom did was look for Jasmine, who was nowhere to be seen. And when Mrs. Bellamy said that she hadn't checked in after school, they both assumed the worst. Mom was a basket case and Mrs. Bellamy wasn't much better.

So when Jasmine came strolling up the street, licking the drips off an ice-cream cone, they were both ecstatic. Mom gave Jasmine a huge hug, holding on to her as if she would never let go.

Once the fire trucks left and all the neighbours went home, though, things really started to get crazy. That's when Jasmine told Mom that she wasn't in the garage because she'd gone off with a stranger.

This little piece of news sent Mom right through the roof. And when Jasmine tried to calm her down by explaining that she only went with the woman because that's what Mom wanted, it just made things worse. In fact, Mom totally lost it.

She was sure Jasmine was making up the whole story to get out of explaining where she'd really been after school. She accused her of lying and sent her to bed right after dinner.

"When you're ready to tell the truth, young lady, you can come downstairs again," she said grimly.

What with Jasmine bawling in her room and Mom slamming dishes and pots around in the kitchen, the house was pretty tense. So I decided that it was time to step in and persuade Jasmine to come clean. And that's how I ended up sitting on the end of her bed listening to a really strange story.

"Vinnie," she said, snuffling into a soggy Kleenex, "the lady came up to me at the schoolyard gate and said Mom wanted me to go with her. She said, 'Unicorn,' so I knew it was okay."

"Unicorn" is our password. Mom picked it because she loves unicorns. She has lots of them. She used to collect them when she was young. She has two stuffed ones, a plastic one, a poster of one, a silver one, and her favourite — a tiny crystal one that sits on her dresser. Jasmine's always holding it up at the window so the sun can shine through it and make rainbows dance on the wall. But she's really careful because she knows how much Mom likes it.

Jasmine also said that the woman knew a lot about Mom. "She knew lots of stuff, Vinnie. She knew Mom likes black cherry ice cream and cheeseburgers and red flowers."

"Did the lady say how she knew this stuff?"

"Nope," Jasmine answered miserably.

"Well, what did she say?"

Jasmine blew her nose again. "Well, at the park, when we passed the roses, she asked if Mom still loves the red ones best."

"Wait a minute," I interrupted. "Are you sure she said 'still loves the red ones?'"

Jasmine nodded.

"Now think hard, Jasmine. Try to remember exactly what she said when you first saw her."

"She was over by the gate and she said my name and I went over. Then she said, 'Your mom wants you to come with me.' So I asked her for the pass-word, like I'm supposed to, and the lady just smiled . . . and then she said it. 'Unicorn.' So I went with her . . . to the park . . . and then to the ice cream store and . . ."

"Hold on, back up a minute. Did your friends see the lady at school?"

"I dunno. Maybe."

"Well, didn't you explain why you weren't walking home with them?"

"Nope, I already told them I was going to run home by myself."

"Why?"

"'Cause I wanted to glue the sparkly stuff on the popsicle-stick box I made for Mrs. Bellamy. I left it on the table in the garage last night and I wanted to finish it and give it to her. It was supposed to be a surprise."

My stomach tightened. "Jasmine, do you understand what a close call this was? Do you know what would have happened if you'd gone to the garage like you planned?"

"I know, Vinnie," she howled. "But I didn't and I didn't burn up because I went with the lady."

Jasmine was pretty convincing. Besides, if she was going to make up a lie, why would she pick such a stupid one? One Mom and I would see right through the minute she opened her mouth?

I decided that I believed her. But I needed to find a way to convince Mom. If I could find out who the woman was, then Mom could check Jasmine's story with her — and the mystery would be solved. But I needed more information.

"Okay, Jasmine, who saw you with the lady? Maybe some other kids in the park? Or maybe the man at the ice cream store?"

Jasmine shrugged glumly. "I don't know. The lady gave me the money for the ice cream — a double scooper — and waited for me outside on that little white bench. You know the one I mean?"

I nodded, then had another thought.

"You mentioned cheeseburgers. Did you go for a cheeseburger? Did someone see you there?"

"Nope. I still had my ice cream. When we passed Best Fries, the lady asked me if I liked cheeseburgers, just like Mom. I said yes and she asked if I wanted one. But I still had my ice cream and, besides, I said I'd be too full to eat dinner. That's when she disappeared."

"Disappeared? You never said anything about her disappearing before."

"Well, you never asked me."

"Okay, so I'm asking now. What happened?"

"Well, when I said the stuff about being too full to eat dinner, the lady looked at her watch. Then she said, 'I think you've been gone long enough,' and then I saw Vanessa and . . ."

"Hold on," I interrupted. "She said, 'You've been gone long enough'? You're sure that's what she said?"

"I'm sure."

I was confused. Why, I wondered, would the woman say something like that? Long enough for what? It didn't make any sense. Neither did the bit about her disappearing. Could

Mom be right after all? Was Jasmine making it all up?

"All right. Go on. You saw Vanessa and then what?"

"Vanessa was across the street with her mom, so I waved and showed her my ice cream. And when I turned around again, the lady was gone. She was just . . . gone. So I came home . . . and the garage was on fire and Mom was crying and hugging me. And then later, she said I was lying and . . ."

Jasmine started bawling again. I waited until she calmed down a little, then tucked her in.

"Go to sleep now, you hear?" I said. She peeked out over the sheet and nodded.

As I was getting up to leave, I thought of one more question.

"Jasmine, what was the lady's name?"

Jasmine gave a little shrug.

"Didn't she tell you? Didn't she say 'Hi, I'm so-and-so' or something?"

"I forget," Jasmine whispered, rolling over to face the wall, "and I'm too tired to remember . . ."

The next morning, the house was still pretty miserable. Jasmine's eyes were swollen from all the crying she'd done and Mom was still pretty grim.

When I got home from school, I slipped up to Mom's bedroom and called some of Jasmine's friends to ask if they'd seen her with a stranger. The only clue I got was from Carla Muir.

"No, I didn't see Jasmine with anybody," she said. "The last time I saw her, she was standing at the gate of the schoolyard and then she just walked away by herself."

I went downstairs and found Jasmine at the kitchen table, her math workbook open in front of her. She was staring out the window, watching Karen and David Bellamy playing in the driveway.

"Want a popsicle?" I asked, opening the freezer.

"Nope."

"Suit yourself, but I've got a question. Remember yesterday when the lady met you at the gate?"

Jasmine nodded, but didn't look up.

"Well, how long did you wait before she came along?"

"She was there when I came out."

I was getting frustrated. "Look, Jasmine. Carla just told me she saw you at the gate — by yourself."

"I wasn't by myself," Jasmine said stonily. "The lady was there. I was talking to the lady."

Her face screwed up and I could tell the tears were about to flow again. I threw up my hands and went back upstairs. Jasmine's story wasn't hanging together. I decided to make one last phone call. After that, I didn't know what I was going to do.

Vanessa's mother answered on the fourth ring. "Mrs. Hall, do you remember seeing my sister yesterday afternoon, outside Best Fries?"

"Oh, yes. Vanessa and I were on the way to the library. Her books were overdue."

Finally, I thought. Now I could get some answers about the mysterious stranger.

"Did you happen to notice who she was with, Mrs. Hall?"

"Who she was with? She wasn't with anyone, Vinnie. She was just standing there, by herself, eating an ice cream cone."

"She wasn't with a woman?"

"No . . . but, wait, let me think . . . maybe there was

someone inside the restaurant. Jasmine did seem to be talking to someone, though I couldn't see who it was. She was waving her ice cream cone around and smiling."

"That's great, Mrs. Hall. Can you remember anything else?"

"Not really. Jasmine just waved to us, then stood there looking around. Then she walked away. Why are you asking all these questions?"

"Oh, it's nothing, Mrs. Hall."

I thanked her and got off the phone. But I wondered why I'd said thank you. What I'd just heard left me more uncertain than ever. If Jasmine had gone off with someone, she was the only one who had seen her. Either that, or Jasmine had started talking to herself in a big way. Somehow, the mess I'd set out to clear up was becoming more muddled than ever.

Later that night, after Jasmine was in bed, I told Mom what I'd found out. She was puzzled, too. We went round and round in "maybe" circles — maybe Jasmine did this, maybe she did that, maybe she, maybe, maybe, maybe. Nothing made sense. Finally, Mom came up with one more "maybe."

"Vinnie, maybe Jasmine just imagined the lady, like little kids sometimes imagine a playmate. I did when I was little. And so did Dawn. You remember me telling you about Dawn?"

Mom paused for a moment, lost in thought. She hadn't mentioned her best friend, Dawn, in years. Not since she'd gotten the news that Dawn and her two little boys had died in a fire. Jasmine had been a baby at the time and Dad had still been around, too.

I remember the day the letter arrived. I came home from school and Dad was there, holding Jasmine. Mom was sitting on the couch holding the letter and wiping tears from her eyes . . .

Our thoughts leaped back to the present. Mom walked over to the buffet and took her old photograph album from the bottom drawer. She came back to the couch and began slowly turning the pages. Finally, she stopped at a picture of two young girls grinning at the camera, each clutching a stuffed unicorn.

"That's me and that's Dawn. We were ten then. It was amazing, Vinnie. We both loved the same things, even unicorns. Can you believe it? She gave me that little crystal one on my dresser just before she moved to Guatemala."

She flipped to a picture of two young women wearing gowns and mortarboards. They were smiling for the camera and clutching diplomas.

"She was such a special friend, Vinnie. We were always there for each other until . . ."

She stopped when she heard the footsteps on the stairs. Jasmine appeared, rubbing the sleep from her eyes.

"What are you doing up, honey?" Mom asked, motioning for Jasmine to join us on the couch. "Did you have a bad dream?"

Jasmine nodded and snuggled between us. Mom put the photo album on the coffee table and turned to give her a cuddle. But Jasmine suddenly squirmed away.

"You found her, you found her!" she whooped.

"Found who?" Mom asked.

"The lady! There." Jasmine was pointing at the graduation picture of Mom and Dawn. "You found her, didn't you, Vinnie? I knew you would." She threw her arms around my neck.

Stunned, I looked over her head at Mom. Mom stared back at me, then looked back at the picture. Finally, she broke the silence.

"Jasmine, come here," she said, patting her lap. Jasmine shifted over. "Now, look at me. Are you saying this is the lady you went with after school?"

"Yes, yes, yes!" Jasmine bubbled.

This time, it was Mom who looked over Jasmine's head at me. She looked confused, maybe even a little frightened. I know that's how I felt. I felt goosebumps on my neck. Had Dawn really come back from the grave to save my little sister?

Jasmine looked up at Mom.

"Mom? She's your friend, isn't she? You just forgot about her, didn't you?"

"You're right, Jasmine," she said softly. "I just forgot about her. She was a very special friend. Now, it's way past your bedtime. But I promise, I'll tell you all about her one day."

THE NEWCOMER

Raffi knew exactly how it felt to be the new kid. He remembered his own first day at Langley — and how nervous he'd been. So when he spotted Damien, all alone, leaning against the schoolyard fence, he walked over.

"Hi," he said, trying to sound friendly, but not pushy. "I'm Raffi Kadir."

"Hi, I'm Raffi Kadir," Damien repeated snarkily.

Startled, Raffi blurted, "What's the matter with you?"

"What's the matter with you?" Damien parroted.

"Hey, come on. I was just trying to . . ."

Before Raffi finished, Damien was already repeating his words, like an evil echo. Turning away, Raffi muttered, "Forget it."

He flinched as Damien spat back, "Forget it."

"So . . . what's he like?" Tony Lo Presti asked as Raffi rejoined the cluster of kids gathered near the door. Tony glanced warily at Damien before continuing. "Did you ask where he came from?"

"Nope," Raffi shrugged.

When Mrs. Mullen had introduced Damien to the class and asked him to say something about himself, he'd simply shaken his head. At the time, Raffi had thought that the newcomer was just shy. Now he wasn't so sure.

"Melanie says he just stared at her when she tried to talk to him," Jenny Clayton added in a low voice. "Remember when she was handing out the magnifying glasses? She says he's scary."

"So?" Raffi said, trying to sound calmer than he felt. "People say lots of things about a new kid, right?"

"Yeah, but . . ." Tony argued, "this guy could be trouble. I mean, look at what he's doing right now." He added quickly, "But don't stare."

Damien had grabbed a soccer ball from a group of grade three kids. He was holding it at arm's length, out of their reach. One boy jumped up and grabbed Damien's arm, trying to drag it and the ball down. Damien shook him off like a fly. Then he drew back his arm and heaved the ball all the way to the far end of the yard.

At that moment, the bell rang and everyone, including Damien, started toward the door.

By lunchtime, Raffi had nearly forgotten the nastiness at recess. So it took him a while to catch on to what was happening behind his back as he walked to the cafeteria.

First, he noticed two little kids outside Miss Daneff's room staring past him. Then, he heard the giggling. He turned quickly, and caught Damien turning too, just a few steps behind him. Three grade-eight girls farther back snickered.

A feeling of helplessness washed over Raffi. He knew exactly what would happen the instant he turned around again. Damien would follow him, imitating everything he did.

"What's with you?" Raffi asked.

"What's with you?" Damien repeated, without turning to face Raffi.

Quickly, Raffi moved toward Damien and stepped in front of him. "I was just trying to be friendly. Guess I was stupid, eh?"

Without waiting, he strode deliberately past his tormentor to the cafeteria. As he pushed open the door, he enjoyed a brief moment of satisfaction. Damien had made it all the way to "stupid" before he caught on.

But Raffi's victory was fleeting. During lunch, Damien positioned himself at the next table and mirrored his every move. He even managed to win over a small audience of nervous grade fives desperate to avoid becoming victims themselves.

During afternoon classes, Damien toned down the attack somewhat. But even though the teacher noticed nothing unusual, Raffi knew what was going on behind his back. And he felt powerless to combat it.

The next two days were Raffi's worst ever at Langley. His only defense was to keep away from the tall, glowering newcomer whenever he could and to say as little as possible. He even stopped putting up his hand to answer questions for fear of hearing the vicious whisper mimicking his words from two seats back and one over.

When his friends asked him what he was going to do, he shrugged and told them he could handle it. Sounding more confident than he felt, he said that Damien would soon get bored with his stupid game and everything would be fine again.

"Maybe you should tell Mrs. Mullen," Jenny suggested.

Tony rolled his eyes, saying that would probably only make matters worse.

But Jenny persisted. "Mrs. Mullen says she won't stand for bullying, and this is bullying, that's for sure. I bet she can help."

"Maybe," Raffi agreed, "but Tony's probably right. Anyway, what am I going to say? That Damien is driving me crazy by acting like my shadow? I'll sound like an idiot."

"She'd understand."

"Maybe, but he wouldn't," Tony shot back. "What do you say we get some of the guys together and make him understand?"

The thought of beating up someone horrified Raffi, but he didn't say so. Instead he simply repeated that he could take whatever Damien was dishing out.

"Well, I couldn't," Jenny admitted. "I still think you should tell Mrs. Mullen. She'd understand. Or how about your mom or dad? They would too, I bet."

By Friday, however, Raffi doubted whether Mrs. Mullen or his parents would understand what was happening between him and Damien. He didn't think anyone would. Why should they, he thought. It was impossible.

Impossible as it seemed, though, Raffi was convinced that Damien was no longer just one nerve-racking step behind him. He was now a sinister sidekick, lifting a hand exactly when Raffi did, reaching for a sandwich or opening his locker at exactly the same moment, even saying or whispering the few words that Raffi still spoke in exactly the same breath. There was no longer a time delay on the bully's broadcast network.

After school on Friday, Raffi hid in the washroom until he figured the coast was clear. Then, he slipped out of the building and, like a lone rider waiting to be ambushed, cautiously worked his way home.

The dreaded Damien never materialized. Raffi made it safely to his house but, even after slamming the door behind him, he didn't feel safe. Shaded windows and thick brick walls were useless barriers against someone who seemed to be able to tune in his thoughts at will. Raffi tossed his bag behind the coat rack and threw himself on the couch, face down.

That's where his dad found him a few minutes later.

"I thought I heard you come in," Mr. Kadir said. "Here, look at this one."

Raffi glanced at the watch his dad was holding out. The back was open and he could see the tiny brass wheels and gears turning smoothly.

"Isn't it a beauty?" Mr. Kadir continued. "Lucy Vanier brought it in yesterday. It was her great-great-grand-father's. I couldn't resist working on it right away. Just one little spring — that's all it needed. And now it's ticking away like new again."

"Just a spring, eh?" Raffi asked, trying to sound interested in the work that brought his dad such satisfaction.

"That's all. She wound it too tight by mistake, and it just snapped."

I know how that feels, Raffi thought, watching his dad's long, thick fingers gently close the watch. It never ceased to amaze him that a man with such big hands could do such delicate work.

Mr. Kadir palmed the watch in his left hand and reached out with the other to brush the hair off Raffi's forehead. He frowned and asked, "Everything okay, son?"

Raffi rolled over, hoping his eyes wouldn't betray the turmoil he felt.

"I'm fine, Dad. Leave me alone, okay? I'm just tired."

"And a bit touchy too, eh? Your mom won't be home from work for another hour. Why don't you grab a nap? I'll be down in the shop if you need me."

"Sounds good," Raffi mumbled, turning his face back into the cushion.

"I'm beat," he added, shutting his eyes. Within a few minutes he was lost in sleep, but it was a sleep that brought him no rest.

The dream was painfully real. He was running — from a monstrous, twisted version of Damien that was reaching toward him with long, talon-like fingers. "You can't get away, Raffi," it intoned as it drew ever closer. "There's plenty of room in here for me," it said as the hands began to claw at Raffi's hair. "I'm coming in."

Raffi woke with a start. He was sweating and gasping for breath, as if he had actually been running. He sat up and leaned against the back of the couch, trying to calm down. Some of the nightmare's details were already fading, but not the fear it had created — and not Damien's words.

"You can't come in," Raffi whispered to the empty room. But, he wondered as he pushed himself up, how do I keep

him out? Feeling helpless, Raffi dragged himself into the kitchen, toward the comforting sound of his parents' voices and dishes rattling. He couldn't stand another minute alone.

Miserable as he was, Raffi told his parents nothing, not even when his mother asked straight out if something was bothering him. Instead, he mumbled that he felt crummy and said he'd decided to go to bed early.

He didn't like lying, but he knew exactly how they'd react if he told them the truth. They'd be worried and angry and they'd probably want to call the principal. That's all I need, he thought, as he headed upstairs. My parents talking to the principal. Then the whole school will think I'm a wimp.

As he slipped under the covers, he decided he'd just have to wait until Damien stopped.

But, as he surrendered to an overwhelming fatigue, Raffi was haunted by the thought that Damien would never stop. Damien would go on and on, until he got what he wanted — whatever that was. Then he'd find another victim and the vicious game would start all over again.

Raffi managed to survive the rest of the weekend without arousing his parents' suspicions that anything really serious might be wrong. When Tony dropped by Saturday afternoon to see if he wanted to shoot some baskets, he said he was still feeling too crummy.

And he dredged up the too-much-homework routine to avoid joining the kids on a visit to the new virtual reality exhibit at the Science Centre. This was hard to pass up, but keeping out of Damien's line of fire was the only defense he felt he had. Besides, he wasn't sure he could stomach any more virtual reality than he was already experiencing. Damien couldn't be real. Real people couldn't do what he did.

Monday morning brought with it the harsh realization that hiding out was no longer an option. Filled with dread, Raffi dressed slowly, dragging on a clean pair of jeans, an old green T-shirt and his well-worn Leafs cap. Halfway through his Shreddies, the knot building in his stomach tightened and he put down his spoon, unable to take another bite.

After pouring the leftover cereal down the sink when his dad wasn't looking, he moved to the hall, picked up his bag and opened the door. As it closed behind him, he called out a quick goodbye. He had to get away before his parents saw the look he was sure must be in his eyes, the haunted look of someone trapped in a hopeless situation. Shoulders sagging, he set out for school.

It wasn't until he wandered into his homeroom two minutes after the bell rang that he realized the full extent of Damien's power. As he passed the seat two behind and one over from his, a flash of green caught his eye. There was Damien, smirking. He was wearing blue jeans, a green T-shirt and a well-worn Leafs cap.

Before Raffi could gasp, Damien beat him to it. Then he said, "We're wearing the same clothes."

Raffi was horrified. The same words had just flashed through his own mind. It had finally happened. His nightmare had come true. Damien was in his head, thinking his thoughts, making the same choices he did.

Like a deer frozen in a spotlight, Raffi stood in the aisle, his breath coming in short gasps. His eyes blurred and tears began to scald his cheeks. Humiliated, he turned and ran from the classroom, ignoring Mrs. Mullen's plea to stop.

His mother had left for work when Raffi arrived back home, but the squeaky floorboards in the hall gave him away. From his repair shop in the basement, his father called out loudly, "Who's there?"

"Just me, Dad," Raffi called back, trying to stop his voice from cracking. "Feeling sick again. Going to bed. That's all."

Raffi made it all the way to his room and into bed before he heard the phone. It rang just once. Good, he thought, figuring a customer's call would distract his father. But, moments later, his dad was standing in the doorway.

"Raffi, that was Mrs. Mullen. What happened?"

Fighting for control, Raffi outlined his torment. He told his dad about Damien and the laughter of the other kids. He didn't — he couldn't — tell him about how Damien had finally invaded his mind. Instead, afraid to say more, he clenched his fist and began punching his pillow.

"Bet you wish that pillow was him," Dad said softly, sitting on the bed beside him.

Raffi nodded weakly.

"Bullies can do that to you — make you want to punch their faces in. But that's not you, is it?"

Raffi nodded again and gave the pillow a last feeble punch.

"Or they make you run and hide. Either way, they've got you, right? The turf is theirs. They just take over."

Mr. Kadir placed his hand on Raffi's shoulder. "Look at me, son."

Raffi looked up at his dad.

"Do you want me to go back to school with you?" Raffi shook his head.

"Okay. Then how about talking to Mrs. Mullen? She's

worried about you and I know she could help."

Again, Raffi shook his head.

"All right. Maybe what you need right now is time, time to think this through. But promise me one thing. Promise me you'll ask for help if you need it. That's the other way a bully gets you, by making you afraid to do that. Promise?"

Raffi promised and, after letting his dad tuck the covers around him, lay alone and exhausted, staring blankly at the ceiling. In his mind, he replayed the horrors of the last week. Like a movie playing backwards, he started with Damien's ghoulish triumph an hour earlier and worked back through the less deadly days of shadow-dancing to the petty parroting that had started it all off last Monday.

At this point, Raffi hit his mental pause button. He managed a small smile when he recalled how he had nearly trapped Damien into saying, "Guess I was stupid."

Damien had seemed human enough that day, with his evil powers still under wraps. Maybe, Raffi wondered, I could have stopped him back then, done something, told somebody. But it was too late now. Damien's powers had been revealed and, as if feeding on something, they were growing stronger.

Raffi froze this frame for a moment. He approached it carefully, poking at it to see if it would snarl and poke back. It didn't. It lay still in his head, waiting for him to make sense of it. When he did, a glimmer of hope and the vague outline of a plan emerged from his frustration and desperation.

Raffi pushed himself up and sat on the edge of the bed, letting his plan take shape. When he had filled in a few missing details, he still wasn't sure it would work. But he was sure of one thing — he had to give it a try.

He considered changing his clothes, but quickly dismissed this idea. "I can wear what I want," he said aloud as he stood up.

He jammed his feet into his sneakers, grabbed his cap from the bed and headed downstairs. He walked over to the bench where his dad was working on an old mantel clock.

"Feeling better, son?" Mr. Kadir began, but Raffi interrupted.

"Dad, I know this is going to sound really weird, but I've got to ask you something. Would you call Mrs. Mullen for me?"

"No problem. I'm sure she'll have a talk with this kid and . . ."

"No, Dad. No. That's not what I want. Please, could you just call her and tell her I'm on my way back to school — and ask her not to say a word when I walk in?"

"Of course," Dad said guardedly. "But you're not going to do anything foolish?"

Knowing what Dad was afraid of, Raffi reassured him with a grin, saying quickly, "Don't worry, Dad. That's not me, remember?"

As he bounded up the stairs and out of the house, he added, "You can tell her if I need her help, I'll ask for it, okay?"

"You will?"

"I will, Dad, for sure."

The fear Damien created was still with him when

Raffi reached the school, but he was no longer fighting it. Instead, he was counting on it to act as a distraction. If his plan worked, Damien would be so busy feeding on that fear that he wouldn't realize what was happening.

He paused at the school door, took a deep breath and walked in. He passed the office and headed down the long hall to his homeroom. As he got closer, he saw that the door was open.

When he slipped into the back of the classroom, Mrs. Mullen stared at him for a moment, as if to make sure of something. Then she looked back at the class without saying a word.

Raffi stood perfectly still and focused on the desk two back and one over from his own. He gauged the distance between himself and his desk, and between Damien and Mrs. Mullen. Then he concentrated fiercely. Nothing happened.

Frantic, Raffi tightened every muscle in his body and concentrated even harder.

At last, Damien started to move. Slowly, he stood up and took a step forward. Raffi did the same. The rest of the class — and Mrs. Mullen — watched in silence.

Step after step, Raffi followed — until Damien stopped in front of Mrs. Mullen. Raffi stopped, too, right beside his own desk. Then he focused on each word of the silent speech he'd prepared.

Damien's words sounded wooden, almost mechanical, but they were loud and clear.

"Damien is a bully, but he's not going to win. Raffi is fighting back. Damien is a bully, but he's not going to . . ."

The snickers came first, followed by giggles. Then Tony blurted out, "Right on!" and the clapping started.

His face twisted with rage, Damien swung around to face the class. His mouth moved, but no words came out. He lurched forward and headed down the aisle. Raffi stepped aside to let him pass. The slamming of the door echoed off the walls, then the room went quiet.

Like a spring that's wound too tight, then released, Raffi suddenly felt weak. His legs went slack and he slumped into his seat, blushing slightly. How, he thought, am I ever going to explain this?

As if reading his mind, Mrs. Mullen called the class to order, adding, "Let's give Raffi some time to unwind. We'll talk about this later."

Raffi grinned his thanks. He had no idea what he was going to say when everyone started asking questions, but at least he'd have time to think about it. And since he was thinking for himself again, he figured he might come up with some pretty good answers.

NiGHT GAMES

Luke had never stayed home alone at night. And convincing his mom that he was old enough to look after himself for a few hours took some doing.

"I don't like to leave you by yourself way out here. I wish Stephanie were here," she sighed.

"Well, Stephanie's at college now, Mom. She can't just zip home and stay with me. Besides, I'd rather stay alone. Stephanie used to scare me to death. The minute you guys walked out the door, she'd start in about the hideous, slime-covered monsters in the basement."

"She didn't!"

"She did. And that's not all. She'd drag up every scary story she could think of and tell me all the gory details. I'm better off alone. Right, Dad?" Luke appealed to his father.

"Well, we won't be that far away, so I suppose . . ."

Luke grabbed the opening. "See, Mom. Dad thinks I'll be fine, too."

Luke eventually succeeded in wearing her down. But when it was time to go, it took her five minutes to run through a list of what-to-do-ifs . . .

Then she started on the next list. "Now remember, the nachos are in the cupboard over the stove and . . ."

"Mom, I live here, remember?"

"All right," she laughed. "Now, you're sure you remember where I wrote down the phone number you can reach us at?"

"Yes, Mom. It's stuck to the fridge door."

"And one last thing. No one comes over, right?"

"Are you kidding? The action starts as soon as you leave. I told everybody to come over for a plate-breaking party. Which should we start with — the good dishes or the everyday ones?"

"I suppose you think that's funny?" Mom asked, trying to keep a straight face.

"Dad, take her away, please."

His dad obliged and Luke locked the door behind them. Then he let out a whoop, dashed into the living room and dove onto the couch. With no one around to complain, he channel-surfed for nearly an hour.

When he couldn't find anything he wanted to watch at 8:30, he headed for the kitchen. Popcorn, chips or nachos, or maybe even all of them? he asked himself. This is great, he gloated, trying to make up his mind.

He settled on nachos, but not just any old chips straight from the bag. He opened the fridge and got out the cheese, a tomato, two green onions and the salsa. Then he scoured the shelves until he came up with a tin of colossal-sized black olives.

These are going to be amazing, he thought. He was drooling as he chopped, sliced and grated. When the plate was heaped to overflowing, he popped it into the microwave, set the timer to three minutes, and stood back to watch.

He was back in front of the television by 8:59, nachos on his lap. As the opening credits for *Young Samurai* started to roll, he felt on top of the world. This staying alone is a piece of cake, he thought. But seconds later, he was on his feet.

The noise — a scratching, tapping sound — had come from the basement. Luke moved quietly into the hall and stood at the top of the stairs, listening. There it is again, he thought.

His stomach tightened. Visions of Stephanie's slimy monsters sprang into his head.

Maybe I should call the police, he thought. But what if they don't find anything? I'll feel like a jerk — and, for sure, I'll end up having babysitters till I'm twenty.

So what do I do? Do I stay up here, scared out of my mind, or do I go down and find out what it is?

Luke made a decision. "All right," he shouted. "I'm coming down."

He flicked on the light and stomped noisily down the rickety wooden stairs. In the stark glare of the single, naked bulb, the trunks and stacks of boxes cast eerie shadows on the dank stone walls. But that's all Luke saw. Just shadows.

Then his heart stopped. He heard the scratching again, coming from the window. Slowly, he turned toward the sound, fearful of what he'd see.

Holding his breath, he inched closer to the window and peered into the darkness. When he spotted the branch, it wasn't touching the glass. Then it swayed in the wind and scraped against the pane before bouncing back and away.

Luke let out his breath noisily. The lilac bush. Feeling foolish, he headed back upstairs. But he nearly jumped out of his skin when the telephone shrilled right beside him in the hall.

He grabbed the receiver on the second ring. "Hello."

Silence.

"Hello?"

More silence.

"Hey, is anybody there?"

Still more silence.

Luke shrugged as he hung up, then headed back into the living room. But he'd no sooner stuffed a warm chip into his mouth than the phone rang again.

Jumping up, he knocked over the half full can of pop on the table beside him. With one hand, he grabbed the can and righted it. With the other, he slapped a pile of paper napkins on the spill. Then he dashed back into the hall, shouting, "I'm coming. I'm coming."

He got to it on the sixth ring.

"Hello."

Silence.

"Who is this?" he shouted.

More silence.

"Hey, this isn't funny," he yelled, his voice cracking. Still more silence.

"Stop it, jerk," he screamed directly into the receiver, then slammed it down.

As he did, he remembered one of Stephanie's horror stories — about the babysitter who kept getting phone calls. When she answered, a deep, scary voice said only,

"I'm coming to get you." Terrified, she called the police. When they traced the call, they discovered it was coming from another line in the house. The thing on the other end of the line was upstairs all the time.

Luke looked up the stairs, then shook his head. "Thanks a lot, Stephanie," he muttered. "You're nowhere near here and you're still scaring me to death."

Anyway, we don't have a separate line upstairs. Stop being an idiot, he told himself. It's probably just one of my so-called friends.

That's it. He felt better. The phone calls suddenly made sense.

Ryan had called earlier that afternoon to invite him over after dinner to watch a movie with him and Chris and Sanjay. He'd been tempted, but the thought of staying alone for the first time had won out. Besides, he wasn't all that crazy about Chris.

So he told Ryan he couldn't because his folks were going out and wouldn't be around to drive him home.

Telling Ryan this had obviously been a big mistake. Ryan must have told Sanjay and Chris why he hadn't joined them.

He could imagine the scene at the other end of the line — Chris dialing, and the other two smothering their laughter as he screamed, "Who's there?" He was guilty of making a few crank calls himself, so he knew that it could be fun. But not if you were on the receiving end. He'd learned that much tonight.

Still, now that he knew who was calling, he wasn't nervous anymore. He decided to turn the tables on the pranksters. He opened the junk drawer and dug out his sister's old lifeguard's whistle. Then he sat by the phone and waited, ready to answer their ring with one of his own.

He waited and waited. Nothing. Finally, he headed back to the living room to rescue his abandoned nachos. As he picked up the plate, he froze. He was sure he heard the scraping sound again, only this time it was coming from the kitchen. He moved quietly into the hall and listened. Nothing. He waited for what seemed like an eternity. Still nothing.

Stephanie, this is all your fault, he thought as he walked into the kitchen to pop the nachos back into the microwave for a quick warm-up. He saw the face just as he was pulling the plate out again.

Red eyes smouldering and long, sharp fangs bared in a horrible grimace, it was peering in the window. Then, as quickly as it had appeared, it was gone.

Nothing Stephanie had invented could have prepared him for this. Luke opened his mouth and screamed — and nearly dropped the plate. As he tried to juggle it, runny cheese and hot salsa splattered his hands. He dumped the plate on the counter and frantically wiped the burning splashes on his jeans.

He didn't want to, but he knew he had to look back at the window. All he saw was his own terrified face reflected in the dark glass.

Okay, okay, calm down, he urged himself. There was probably nothing there in the first place. It was my own reflection all along. But I don't look that bad. Nobody looks that bad, unless they're wearing a really gross mask.

Mask. That's it, he convinced himself. It was a mask, and I bet I know who was behind it. No wonder those guys never called back. How could they, if they were on their way over here to scare me again?

This is Chris's dirty work, he thought. And he'll love telling everybody at school how I nearly wet my pants when I saw that mask. Boy, am I done for.

Suddenly, the scratching started again. It was coming from the living room.

Luke tiptoed out of the kitchen and down the hall. Tap, tap, tap. He reached around the doorway to switch off the living-room light. The television filled the room with an eerie glow, but Luke wasn't afraid this time. He knew who was at the window and he intended to pay them back.

Tap, tap, scratch, scratch. The noise continued, louder now. It sounded like they were trying to get in. Stealthily, Luke slipped past the couch and around the coffee table. Then, very carefully, he moved over to the drapes covering the big double windows.

The sounds were coming from the window on the right. Slowly, Luke slipped his hand between the drapes and quietly released the lock. Then he carefully pulled back his hand and pressed himself against the wall. He opened the drapes a crack, then held his breath and waited.

It was very dark outside. He could barely make out the shadow slinking toward the window, but he couldn't miss the movement. He waited. The window inched open, then a dark shape reached under the frame and began to push upward.

At that moment, Luke struck. Throwing open the drape, he slammed the window down. He heard a terrible shriek, followed by a strangled whimper.

Horrified, Luke stepped back and let the drape fall into place. Oh no, he thought. What have I done? What if I broke his hand?

Frightened and confused, he backed away, waiting for Chris, Sanjay and Ryan to start yelling at him. But all he heard was more whimpering and a muffled scratching sound.

The ringing of the telephone shattered the silence. Hoping it was Mom or Dad, Luke dashed to answer. His hand shook as he picked up the receiver.

"Hello," he croaked.

"Hey, Luke. Listen, I'm sorry about the phone calls."

"Ryan? Is that you?"

"Yeah. Listen, it was Chris's idea, okay?"

"Ryan . . . where are you now?"

"I'm at home. Where do you think I am?"

"But Chris and Sanjay are gone, right?"

"Nah, they're downstairs. I just came up to get some more chips and I thought I'd let you know it was us, just in case you hadn't figured it out yet. Listen. I gotta go. I'll call you tomorrow."

"Wait, Ryan, don't hang up," Luke whispered hoarsely, but he was too late. The line was dead.

Slowly, he replaced the receiver. Then he turned and stared wide-eyed into the shadows of the living room. Weak with fear, he slumped against the post at the bottom of the stairs.

Stay calm, he ordered, but his body wasn't listening. His heart felt like a jackhammer and the blood pounded in his head. Stop it. Stop it, he commanded. Calm down and call Mom and Dad.

He reached for the phone, then froze. The number was stuck on the fridge. And the living-room window was still unlocked. His skin turned to gooseflesh. Whatever was out there might get in while he was in the kitchen.

Terrified, Luke put down the receiver and looked around for a weapon. His baseball bat was leaning against the wall. Gripping it in both hands, he stepped into the living room and moved quickly to the window. Summoning his last ounce of courage, he yanked the drapes open and jumped back, ready to lash out with the bat.

Seeing nothing, he banged the lock back into place. With a sigh of relief, he reached over to draw the drapes again. As he did, his hand brushed something wet and slimy.

Recoiling, Luke dropped the bat and staggered into the hall. He held up his hand. Green slime dripped down his arm.

Luke's knees turned to jelly and he collapsed in a heap on the floor.

That's where his parents found him ten minutes later, still wiping his hand on his jeans and muttering, "This is your fault, Stephanie. Your fault. No fair."

SPELLBOUND

When the old car pulling a battered silver trailer chugged slowly up the long hill to the Oakley house that day in mid-October, it took about five minutes for the news to get around town. The rundown house had been empty for so long that everyone said it was haunted. Now, the whole town was curious to know who on earth would move in — and why.

Joey Dean and Mario Spinelli took it upon themselves to be the first to find out. Quietly, the two boys worked their way up the rutted lane. Crouching low behind the overgrown bushes that were threatening to take over the weed-choked yard, they stole to the rear of the house and hid beside a ramshackle shed.

From there, they had a clear view of the trailer and the weather-beaten porch that clung precariously to the back of the house. Undetected, they watched the comings and goings of three people — a man, a woman, and a girl — as they shifted boxes, bags and a few suitcases into the house.

"So, they really are moving in," Joey whispered. "But who'd want to live here?"

"Yeah, this place gives me the major creeps," Mario whispered back. "And so do they, right?" he added.

Joey looked at the strangers. They were standing on the porch, gazing out across the hill at the deep rose and purple of a darkening autumn sky. The girl, her face eerily pale in the fading light, was wearing a long black skirt sprinkled with yellow stars. The woman had on a colourful poncho and the man's shoulder-length hair hung down from under a black hat with a wide, bent brim.

Joey shrugged. Mario was right. They did look a little strange. "Well, they're . . . different," he said noncommittally.

"The guy's got long hair. My dad says that's how you can spot weirdos a mile away. And look at that skirt. They must be related to the Addams family." Mario giggled at his own joke.

Suddenly, the girl called out, "Hey, Dad. Look."

"It's a bit late in the year for that fellow to be out," the man said, as the girl picked up what looked like a twisting, dancing piece of rope. "He must have found a warm spot here under the steps."

"See that?" Mario hissed, and elbowed Joey in the ribs. "They like snakes. For sure, they're going to . . ."

He stopped in mid-sentence, interrupted by a rustling in the bushes behind them. Startled, the two boys turned. When the black-and-white shape emerged, Mario bolted.

As his friend crashed noisily through the undergrowth, Joey heard the man call out, "Who's there?"

Joey hesitated just long enough to see the skunk's tail shoot up like a flag, then he took off after Mario.

He caught up with him at the bottom of the hill.

"That was close," Mario panted. "It nearly got us."

"Well, it wouldn't have done anything if you'd just stayed still," Joey protested.

"Says who?" Mario snarled.

Says me, Joey thought, but he knew better than to argue with Mario. Mario was a pretty good friend — as long as he got his own way. Worried that he might have already crossed the line, Joey fell in behind him without saying another word.

They were both out of breath when they reached the Burger Barn, but that didn't stop Mario. He gasped dramatically as he burst through the doors, staggering and clutching his chest as if he'd just outraced a slavering wolf.

"What's with you?" Paula Stroud called.

That was the only cue Mario needed. As Paula and the other kids gathered round, he launched into his tale. The strangers on the porch became snake-charming, spell-casting, bloodsucking, shrieking maniacs who had pursued the two boys down the hill.

Joey enjoyed the story, too, though he objected feebly when Mario reported that the girl had tried to bite off the snake's head. But no one paid any attention, anyway. And when he tried to interrupt again, Mario warned him off with a look that said, Keep your mouth shut.

"We were lucky to get away," Mario finished, his face flushed. He was playing up to every squeal of horror from his audience.

Over the weekend, Mario's tale spread quickly — and more rumours were added with each retelling. By the time Monday morning rolled around, the stage was set.

When the girl and her mother walked through the schoolyard gate, the whispering and pointing started immediately.

Mario wasted no time. Separating himself from the group that had gathered round him, he swaggered over to the pair. "Whatcha got in the bag — snake heads?"

The girl looked puzzled. She stared at Mario, then down at her bag, a green cloth carryall with a rainbow stitched across the front.

"Books and pens," she said quietly, pulling a dog-eared notebook out of the bag. "And my lunch," she added, patting a bulge in the bag. Then she smiled and, with her mother, continued walking into the school.

Watching them climb the stairs, Joey felt a pang of guilt. Once again, though, he hid behind his silence. Why, he wondered, do I let Mario drag me into stuff like this? Because Mario rules, that's why. What he says, goes.

The principal showed up later that morning with Lilith Carsons in tow. When he invited her to introduce herself to the class, a stony silence greeted her.

Nervously, Lilith began to explain that her family had come from New Mexico, that she loved reading and animals, and that her parents had been hired by an Oakley heir to spend the next year repairing and restoring the old house. Her eyes lit up when she described how wonderful it would look.

As she spoke, some of the kids began directing skeptical glances at Mario. By the time she finished, he'd lost a few believers. His description just didn't match the person standing before them.

But this didn't stop him. In fact, it was like waving a red flag in front of a bull. There was no way Mario was going to let the truth get in the way of a great story.

"Who ever heard of a name like Lilith?" he asked in a stage whisper as she passed his desk.

The giggles that followed ended abruptly when she turned, looked him straight in the eye, and said simply, "My mother and father. That's two. And now you make three."

Mario blinked and turned away instantly, as if a flash-bulb had just popped in his face.

But as Lilith continued walking, he recovered. Determined not to give up his advantage, he grabbed his head and rolled noisily out of his chair, groaning, "The evil eye. She got me with the evil eye."

Over the next few days, Mario escalated his campaign of lies. When Lilith carefully picked up a small spider in the lunchroom and put it gently out the window, he told everyone within earshot that he'd seen a huge, hairy black one poking out of her bag.

"She collects them for spells," he declared. When she rescued an injured field mouse from the ditch near the school one afternoon and started home with it, Mario pointed out to anyone who would listen that she was taking it home to feed the bats.

"What bats? Where?" Paula squirmed.

"The ones she keeps in the shed," Mario ad libbed.

"No kidding," Gordon Petrie piped up.

"Mario," Joey finally spoke up, "you're nuts."

Mario's eyes flashed. He grabbed Joey by the arm and

pulled him to one side. "What do you think you're doing, Joey?"

"Mario, you know you're spreading garbage."

"Oh yeah? What makes you so sure, Joey?"

"Mario, I was there that first day, remember. I know what really happened."

"So?"

"So, if you don't stop, I'm going to tell everybody the truth — that we took off because we saw a skunk and . . ." Joey stopped short, suddenly realizing what he was doing. He waited for Mario's counterattack, but it didn't come.

Mario just stared. "I don't believe this. She's got just about everybody fooled — including you." He turned abruptly and stormed away.

"I'm right about her. You'll see," he shouted over his shoulder.

Joey was confused. Mario might be pushy sometimes — well, actually, most of the time — but he isn't stupid, he thought. He's sure acting stupid about Lilith, though. People are starting to laugh at him, not her.

She's definitely getting to Mario. But, he admitted, maybe she's getting to me, too. Isn't it because of her that I finally stood up to Mario?

Joey frowned. Could there really be something different . . . something strange . . . about Lilith? He shook his head, banishing the thought.

But the next day, thoughts of spells and spooks and goblins were on everyone's mind, Joey's included. It was Halloween and, around town, the excitement was building. In an attempt to patch things up with Mario, Joey called him to see if they'd be trick-or-treating together as usual. Mario turned him down flat, saying he had better things to do that night.

Joey didn't like the sound of this. What's Mario up to? he wondered. Halloween could be the perfect camouflage for someone looking for trouble. And if Mario was planning something nasty, Lilith was probably his target.

Joey made a quick decision. When dusk fell and the orange pumpkins began to flicker and glow, he was already in place. He was wearing his old glow-in-the-dark skeleton costume, but he'd draped himself in a dark blue sheet so no one would notice him. From his hiding spot across the street at the bottom of the Oakley lane, he watched as a solitary jack-o-lantern, glowing brightly, was perched on the gatepost. He felt sure its invitation would be ignored. No one was likely to test the theory that the house was haunted, especially not on Halloween.

But Joey did see Lilith come down the lane. Once again, she was wearing the flowing black skirt covered in stars. A mask of feathers hid her face and a shimmering, web-like shawl covered her shoulders.

Joey also saw the werewolf, which had been lurking in the shelter of some bushes, slip out of the darkness and start to follow her. Mario had worn the same werewolf costume last year and the year before.

I was right, Joey thought, as the two figures passed him. He's after her. But what is he going to do? Grabbing the hem of his makeshift cloak, he fell into step a safe distance behind them.

The strange, silent parade of three wound up and down

the dimly lit streets. Lilith's bag grew heavier at each stop, but Mario's and Joey's stayed empty. Neither wanted to lose track of his quarry.

Just before Lilith turned back onto Main Street, Mario made his move. He increased his pace and caught up to Lilith in the shadows behind the Burger Barn. He ran up behind her, growling and snarling, and snatched her bag. Then he disappeared around the corner.

Joey was too far behind to do anything. He tried to catch up, but his legs tangled in the sheet. When he finally staggered up to Lilith, she was just standing there slipping the ends of her filmy shawl through her fingers.

"It's me — Joey," he blurted. "Are you all right?"

"Yeah. I'm fine."

"I'll get it back," he offered, still struggling with his costume. "Hold this." He thrust his bag into Lilith's startled hands. "I'll be right back."

"Joey, you don't have to . . ." Lilith began, but Joey was already turning the corner. He heard Mario before he saw him. His strangled scream pierced the night air.

Mario had pulled off his mask and was standing beside the bench in front of the post office. Lilith's bag lay in a crumpled heap at his feet. His face was contorted in horror and, suddenly, he started flailing wildly at his costume.

Joey stopped dead, then jumped back. The bench — and the pavement beneath it — was covered with every creepy-crawly imaginable. Snakes slithered, spiders scuttled, and bugs scattered in all directions, some of them clinging to the fur of Mario's costume. Out of the darkness, bats suddenly swooped around his head.

Trying to duck and brush away the creatures at the same time, Mario looked like he was doing some kind of crazy dance.

Lilith slipped through the small crowd that had gathered to witness the scene and stood next to Joey. When Mario saw her, he froze.

"Get her away from me," he shouted frantically. "She did it. She did it."

"Did what?" Joey asked. "Let you steal her bag, then pretend this stuff was in it?"

"How do you know that I stole . . . ?" Mario stopped. "But wait, that means you saw. You saw what happened. You know what she did."

"I don't know what you're talking about," Joey said, walking away.

He felt the tug on his arm halfway up the street. It was Lilith. She'd taken off her mask. It was dangling on her wrist from a thin white elastic. As the feathers moved, they looked like a strange bird getting ready to take flight.

"You forgot these," Lilith said, holding out the sheet and his loot bag. The bag was full.

Joey started to reach for it, then pulled back his hand. He looked uncomfortably at Lilith, remembering what had happened to Mario.

"Don't worry. It's okay," she smiled knowingly.

Joey took the bag. Carefully, he opened it and reached in. Nothing crawled up his arm. Nothing slithered through his fingers. In fact, the bag was full of familiar shapes.

Joey pulled out two peanut butter cups. "Want one?" he asked.

"Thanks," she said, taking one. "They're my favourites."

"Mine too."

"I know," Lilith said quietly.

LIFE GUARD

Raymond Fortuna held his little sister Angelina's hand as they walked up from the lake. They'd been watching a loon diving for fish and counting how long it could stay underwater before popping up for air.

"Ray Ray," Angelina said when they reached the weather-beaten cabin tucked under the pines. "It's still smelly in here."

"But it's not so bad now," Raymond said, taking a sniff as he held open the screen door. "See, Dad was right. It just needed some fresh air."

"Like us," his father had pointed out when they'd unpacked that morning. "Fresh air, lots and lots of fresh air. So much better than at the apartment. And it's free," Mr. Fortuna had sung out, scooping up Angelina and spinning her around.

"But it still smells a little bit, doesn't it?" Angelina asked as they went into the kitchen.

"You're right. But it's not gross or anything. Just a little musty. So let's not complain to Dad again, okay? He's so happy that he can give us a little holiday at a cottage."

"Okay," Angelina agreed. "Then can we make peanut butter sandwiches now? I want to bring Daddy his lunch in that," she added, pointing to a lime green fruit basket on a shelf beside the fridge.

"Good idea," Raymond said, putting a loaf of sliced bread and two jars on the table. Then he spent the next ten minutes helping Angelina make four very sticky sandwiches, one each for him and her, and the two thickest ones with red jam oozing out the sides for their dad.

"Here," he said, handing her some paper towels. "Wipe your hands with the damp one, and line the basket with the others before you put Dad's sandwiches in it. I'll carry ours and three plates on this tray. And how about some juice boxes?"

"Then it'll be a real picnic. Let's go." Angelina scampered out the door, swinging the basket beside her.

"Daddy, Daddy. Stop working now. We have to have a picnic on this picnic table."

"All right, Angel," Mr. Fortuna said, putting down the circular saw he'd just unloaded from the trunk of the car. "Picnic time it is."

When they finished eating, Raymond and Angelina stayed at the table for a while, watching as their dad lined up, measured and sawed pieces of lumber that had been stored in a shed closer to the water.

"It's like a miracle," Raymond remembered his dad saying a week earlier. "I was asking my boss last night if I could stay home next week because your mother has to go to Montreal when Grandma has her operation and he came up with this great idea. He offered to pay me for the week if I fix up some things at a cottage he has on Pine Lake, and he says the three of us can stay there and have a little vacation at the same time too. Won't that be fun? And he'll even pay for the gas to drive there and back. So I said yes, Raymond. But I'll need your help keeping an eye on Angelina when I'm busy. Okay?" And even though he wasn't thrilled about babysitting for a week, Raymond had said that would be fine.

And now, one week later, he was sitting with his sister by a sparkling lake on a sunny day, a gentle breeze brushing his cheek and, at least so far, everything was fine.

Later that afternoon, while Angelina tracked down ants and dropped them into a jar, Raymond held side posts in place as his dad replaced wobbly parts of the deck railing. When he was no longer needed, he went inside to change into his swimming shorts and get his book. Then he called Angelina in to change too so they'd be ready to go in the water when his dad quit working.

"I unpacked your bag and put your clothes in the drawers," he told her when she came in, "but I left your bathing suit out on the bed."

"Okay, Ray Ray. I'll be right back," she answered as she pushed open the door to her bedroom.

But when she came back out a few minutes later, she still had her shorts and T-shirt on.

"Why didn't you change?" Raymond asked.

"Because the lady with the yellow hair was watching."

"What lady? Where?"

"The lady at the window. In there." Angelina pointed to her room.

Raymond went into the bedroom and looked around. "There's no one here. Come and see."

Angelina went in and stopped near the bed. "Did you look out the window?"

"Yes. Nobody's there. Don't be scared. You were just imagining things. Here," he added, handing her her suit.

"Okay. But I wasn't scared. I was just shy, that's all. Do you miss Mommy? I do. I hope we have hot dogs for dinner. Daddy said he could use the barbeque."

Angelina babbled on and on as she changed, then reached up to Raymond. "Carry me, Ray Ray? I'm not too heavy. I'm still just four and you're ten. Ten is big and you're strong."

Bending down, Raymond told her, "Hop on my back. I'll give you a piggy-back ride. But don't choke me, okay?"

Laughing, Angelina agreed. "I won't. I promise. Let's go."

The rest of the afternoon seemed to fly by. While waiting for their dad to finish up, Raymond helped Angelina build sandcastles. He scooped out deep moats that she kept trying to fill with water and showed her how to build bridges across them with small twigs and leaves. When their dad finally joined them, he did so without warning, suddenly racing past them into the water, clothes and all.

"Yikes, that's a little chilly," he said as he sloshed back to the beach, dripping wet and grinning like a kid from ear to ear. "But I was so sweaty and covered in sawdust that I figured I might as well just jump right in and wash my clothes at the same time." Angelina giggled when she heard this and Raymond gave his dad a thumbs up.

"It's been a long time since Dad looked so happy," he thought as he ran back up to the cottage to get him a towel. "Maybe this week won't be too bad after all."

After time playing in the lake and a dinner of barbequed hot dogs and two-bite brownies, Raymond found himself feeling a little pooped, so he wasn't surprised to see Angelina rubbing her eyes and yawning a lot. And when their dad finally convinced her that his phone wasn't working, she stopped chanting, "I want to talk to Mommy," and agreed to get ready for bed without putting up a fuss.

"She was asleep before I got to page four of *The Mole Sisters*," Mr. Fortuna whispered as he tiptoed back into the kitchen. "And just as well too. I nearly nodded off myself. Will you be all right here for a few minutes while I walk up toward the main road to see if I can get a strong enough signal to phone your mother?"

"Sure," Raymond answered.

"While I'm gone why don't you see if you can find checkers in the top drawer of that old cupboard? I'm thinking we could play a few games on the board painted here," he added, pointing to the black and red squares painted on the wooden kitchen table.

Raymond had dug out all twenty-four checkers and was placing them on the board when he heard the sounds — like very low, muffled words — coming from Angelina's room. He walked quietly down the hall, pushed opened the door and tiptoed toward her bed. In the twilight he could see her curled up on her side, her right arm around her teddy bear, Buttercrunch. She was breathing softly, and she was sound asleep.

I must be hearing things, Raymond thought, looking down at her. Either that or you were talking in your sleep.

But just as he turned to leave, he thought he heard a rustling sound outside the window. He walked over and peered out, but in the greying dusk he saw nothing. And I must be imagining things now too, he told himself as he left the room.

Not wanting to worry his dad, Raymond didn't mention what had happened when he returned. After all, Raymond figured, there really wasn't anything to tell. So he just listened as his dad started talking about the call he had managed to make to Montreal.

"The signal faded in and out a bit, but it wasn't too bad."

"That's good. What did Mom say?"

"She says she misses you a lot and hopes you and Angelina are having fun. And Grandma's going to be fine. The operation went so well they're going to let her leave the hospital tomorrow. And since Auntie Rosa will be back from San Salvador on Thursday, Mom could be back home by the weekend."

"And now," he teased as he sat down at the table, "it's time for less talk and more action. Are you ready to take on the checkers champion of the world?"

But just three games later, Raymond's dad stopped playing.

"Son, I know it's not too late and I should give you another chance to beat me, but I can barely keep my eyes open. All this fresh air must be getting to me," he added, standing up. "Here, give me a hug. I'm off now. But you can stay up and read if you like."

Raymond read for another twenty minutes before he

too headed off to bed. Half asleep already, he crawled under the top sheet without changing into his pyjamas, reaching out to switch off the light on the night table just before sleep closed in on him.

The birds woke him up the next morning. He'd never heard so many chirping all at once like that at the apartment, he thought, opening his eyes to see how bright it was outside. And lying there beside him, wide awake and watching him, was Angelina.

"What are you doing here?" he whispered. "I don't think it's time to get up yet."

"I've been here a long time, Ray Ray," she whispered back. "I came here when it was nighttime to tell you the lady was at the window again and she made me a little scared because she wanted to talk to me. But you were so sleepy you didn't wake up when I poked you and I didn't want to wake up Daddy, so I just stayed here and slept with you. That's okay, isn't it?"

"Of course," Raymond answered softly. "But I think you were just having a bad dream."

"But she said she missed me. Can people talk to you like that in a dream?"

"I've had some dreams with people talking to me in them, so don't worry about it. I tell you what. Let's take this blanket and go sit on that swing seat in the screened-in porch. Maybe we can watch some of those noisy birds from there. Be very quiet and follow me."

"Aren't you the early birds," Mr. Fortuna said when he got up and found them snuggled up on the swing. "Did you two have a good sleep?"

"Yes," Raymond answered for both of them, watching Angelina, and his sister nodded in agreement.

"Then come on in and eat. Cinnamon toast and apple sauce are on the menu this morning. And crunchy granola if that's not enough."

After breakfast, Mr. Fortuna started making new frames for some of the windows, and Raymond and Angelina went back to constructing what Angelina said would be "the best sandcastle village ever." They didn't notice their visitor until the man had pulled his canoe up on to the beach and called out, "Hello."

"Pleased to meet you," he said when Mr. Fortuna walked down and introduced himself.

"I'm Calvin Corbett and I've got a place across the lake," he said, pointing to a clearing in the trees. When I saw your lights on last night, I decided to paddle over this morning. I know Ross Bernier, the owner, and I thought I should see who was here. No one's been here for a long time now, not since the accident . . ." Then he paused.

Mr. Fortuna broke the silence. "We're just here for a week. Ross Bernier is my boss, and he wanted me to spruce up the place a bit. But he didn't say anything about an accident. What accident?"

"Well, he probably finds it harder to rent if he talks about it. But the Benways used to rent here every summer, and three years ago, Carol — the mother — drowned. It was horrible. Fred and Carol and their little girl, Emily, were such a close, loving family, and Carol adored Emily. She was always watching over her like a mother hen. Fred and Emily never came back," he added, slowly shaking his head, "and no one else has stayed here since then."

Angelina had gone back to digging up the sand, but Raymond had been listening closely to what Mr. Corbett had said.

"Excuse me, but you knew those people well, right?" he interrupted.

Mr. Corbett nodded.

"Well, I was just wondering if the lady who drowned had black hair."

"No. She was a blonde."

"Why do you want to know, son?" Mr. Fortuna asked, looking puzzled.

"No reason. I was just wondering. That's all," Raymond answered quickly before going back to Angelina.

Mr. Corbett left soon after, and Mr. Fortuna carried on working.

A little while later, Angelina jumped up and ran toward the cottage. "I have to go to the bathroom," she yelled. "I'll be right back."

But she didn't come right back, so Raymond finally went to see what she was up to. As he opened the door, he heard her say, "Not now. I can't. Go away."

Worried, Raymond went in and found her standing at the kitchen sink. "Who were you talking to?" he demanded.

"The lady, but she's gone again. Don't be mad, Ray Ray. I told her to go away."

"I'm not mad, Angelina. Here, let me get you a drink. And here's an apple. Let's go back outside and eat our apples, okay?"

"Okay. Let's go."

Raymond followed Angelina outside, and sat beside her at the picnic table, not knowing what to do. Should he tell his dad about the mysterious lady? But she can't be real, he told himself, or he would have seen and heard her too. So what should he say? That he was starting to worry because Angelina was imagining too many strange things? That sounded really lame. And maybe his imagination was starting to work overtime too. Why else had he asked Mr. Corbett that question about the drowned lady's hair? No, he ordered himself. Just don't think any more crazy thoughts, keep a close eye on your sister, and everything will be fine.

And everything was fine for the rest of the day. But when Mr. Fortuna headed off to call Montreal after putting Angelina to bed, Raymond thought he heard voices again coming from his sister's room. Just like the night before, when he went in to check on her, she was sound asleep and silence filled the room. But this time, even though it was still hot out, when he passed by the window he felt an icy chill so cold it sent shivers up his spine.

Back in the kitchen, Raymond decided he needed a plan to take care of Angelina during the night that he wouldn't have to tell his dad about. And later, after his dad went to bed, he put his plan into action. Taking his book and a pillow and top sheet from his bed, he tiptoed into Angelina's room. He put the pillow on the floor near the nightlight by her bed, and slid down the wall to sit on it. Then, wrapping the sheet around his shoulders, he picked up his book and started reading by the nightlight's glow.

His plan was to stay awake all night guarding Angelina, but his plan failed.

When he woke up hours later, he was slumped down on the floor, his head halfway on the pillow and the sheet twisted around his legs. Heart beating faster, he pushed himself up on his knees and peered over at Angelina's bed. It was empty. Calm down, he told himself. Maybe she's just gone to the bathroom and that's what woke me up.

He tiptoed down to the bathroom, but she wasn't there. Heart pounding now, he decided to check out the swing on the porch before waking up his dad. She wasn't there either. But just as he turned to head back to his dad's room, he looked out toward the beach, and in the pale light of a breaking dawn he saw her — a small figure with her right arm reaching up as if holding somebody's hand. And she was walking into the water.

"Angelina, no! Come back!" he screamed as he crashed through the door. "Come back!"

The water was nearly up to his sister's neck when he reached the shore.

"Stop, stop," he pleaded as he struggled to reach her, and suddenly she did.

As if in a trance, she looked back at him and said, "She needs me, Ray Ray. She misses me."

By now Raymond had reached his sister. "We need you more," he sobbed as he grabbed her left hand. But something seemed to pull her away from him.

"Let her go!" he cried, looking just past Angelina. "She's not yours. You can't have her."

Just then Raymond's dad pushed past him, snatched up his daughter and waded back to shore. Arms wrapped tightly around her father's neck, she looked down at Raymond and asked, "You saw her, didn't you, Ray Ray?"

"No, I didn't. But I know she was there."

"Who? What are you talking about? And what in the world were you two doing out here anyway?" Mr. Fortuna asked, glaring down at Raymond.

"Don't be mad at Ray Ray, Daddy. Can we go in now? I'm cold."

"So am I," Raymond added, shivering. "I'll try to tell you what happened after I dry off, and maybe you can come up with a better plan to keep Angelina safe. If not, maybe we'll have to go home."

"I miss Mommy," Angelina said as they went inside. "Do you miss her too, Ray Ray? And I like pancakes. Can we have pancakes for breakfast?"

Amazing, Raymond thought as he listened to his little sister chattering. It's as if she's already forgotten what just happened. I wish I could do the same.

But even though he'd never seen her, Raymond knew that no matter how hard he tried to forget Angelina's lady, memories of what she had tried to do to his sister would haunt him for many years to come.

HAUNTED CANADA

READ THE WHOLE CHILLING SERIES

978-0-7791-1410-8

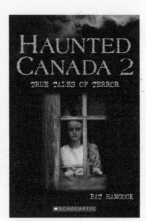

978-0-439-96122-X

978-0-439-93777-1

978-0-545-99314-2

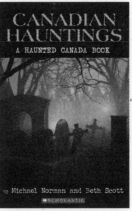

978-0-439-93875-4